"If you're pregnant with my child, that changes things."

"What things, exactly?"

He hesitated. "I'm already engaged to be married."

Her jaw set. "If you got engaged so quickly, you must have known your fiancée."

Gabe parked in her driveway. "No. It was an arranged marriage."

Horror transfixed her. "So that's why you slept with me. It was a last fling."

"It wasn't like that."

"How was it, then?"

His gaze pinned hers for long seconds. "You know exactly how it was between us."

Sarah stared at him, needing to see the truth in his eyes, feeling crazily emotional and on the verge of tears. "So how was it, exactly, between us?"

"Like this." Gabe cupped her jaw and out of nowhere her heart began to pound and the humming, tingling attraction she'd fought to suppress shimmered through her.

He lowered his mouth, and foolishly she tossed away any thoughts of being sensible and controlled and let him kiss her.

Dear Reader,

Some years ago I wrote my first sheikh story, a novella called *Kismet*, which appeared in the Silhouette anthology *Sheiks of Summer* (2002). That story has always been a favorite of mine, and so I couldn't wait to start this story.

But from the first, Sarah would not be quite as I wanted her to be, and neither would Sheikh Kadin Gabriel ben Kadir. The problem was that I still had strong memories of *Kismet*. In order to write Sarah and Gabe's romance, I had to actually purge the past book from my mind.

In a way, Sarah and Gabe faced the same problem in their relationship. The past intruded and tried to dictate what their present should be. Sometimes so strongly, it seemed there was no hope that they could be together. Until Gabe discovered that Sarah was pregnant...and that she was showing every sign of coping quite well without him!

I hope you enjoy,

Fiona Brand

THE SHEIKH'S PREGNANCY PROPOSAL

FIONA BRAND

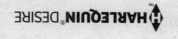

HARLEQUIN® DESIRE

Recycling programs
for this product may
not exist in your area.

ISBN-13: 978-0-373-73387-3

The Sheikh's Pregnancy Proposal

This edition published by arrangement with Harlequin Books S.A.

For questions and comments about the quality of this book, please contact us at CustomerService@Harlequin.com.

® and TM are trademarks of Harlequin Enterprises Limited or its corporate affiliates. Trademarks indicated with ® are registered in the United States Patent and Trademark Office, the Canadian Intellectual Property Office and in other countries.

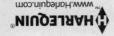 www.Harlequin.com

Printed in U.S.A.

Fiona Brand lives in the sunny Bay of Islands, New Zealand. Now that both her sons are grown, she continues to love writing books and gardening. After a life-changing time in which she met Christ, she has undertaken study for a bachelor of theology and has become a member of The Order of St. Luke, Christ's healing ministry.

Books by Fiona Brand

HARLEQUIN DESIRE

The Sheikh's Pregnancy Proposal

The Pearl House

A Breathless Bride
A Tangled Affair
A Perfect Husband
The Fiancée Charade
Just One More Night

HARLEQUIN ROMANTIC SUSPENSE

O'Halloran's Lady

SILHOUETTE ROMANTIC SUSPENSE

Cullen's Bride
Heart of Midnight
Blade's Lady
Marrying McCabe
Gabriel West: Still the One
High-Stakes Bride

Visit the Author Profile page at
Harlequin.com for more titles!

To the Lord.

"Our Lord showed me an inward sight of His homely loving. I saw that He is everything that is good and comforting to us. He is our clothing. In His love He wraps us and holds us. He enfolds us in love and He will never let us go."
—*The Revelations of Divine Love,* Julian of Norwich

Heartfelt thanks to Stacy Boyd for inspirational suggestions, patience and grace in editing. It's always a joy to work with you.

One

Twenty-four hours away from the deadline to sign a marriage contract…

The stark thought shoved Sheikh Kadin ben Gabriel ben Kadir out of a restless sleep. Tossing crisp linen sheets aside, Gabe flowed to his feet and pulled on a pair of narrow dark jeans. The cool light of a New Zealand dawn flooded his suite, a floor above the Zahiri consulate in Wellington, as he broodingly considered the concept of once more entering into the intimacy of marriage.

Marrying a wealthy heiress would solve his country's financial problems. The problem was, after the disaster of his last marriage, he had no desire to ever immerse himself in that particular hell again.

The morning air cool against his torso, he padded barefoot to the French doors and dragged aside heavy linen curtains. Dark gaze somber, he surveyed the gray rain drenching his last day of bachelor freedom. At that moment, like a fiery omen, the sun pierced the thick veil of storm clouds that hung over Wellington Harbour, illuminating a large painting of his twelfth-century ancestors, which dominated one wall of his suite.

Gabe studied the painting of the original Sheikh Kadin on whose birthday he'd had the bad luck to be born. A battle-hardened Templar Knight, Kadin's main claim to fame was that he had taken someone else's bride along with her diamond-encrusted dowry. The captured bride, Camille de Vallois, a slim redhead with dark exotic eyes, had then proceeded to entrance his ancestor to the point of obsession. Gabe's stomach tightened at the remembrance of the obsession that had haunted his own youthful marriage, although in his case the possessive intensity hadn't emanated from him.

Once they were married, Jasmine, his childhood sweetheart, had become increasingly clingy and demanding, dissolving into tears or throwing tantrums when she didn't get her way. She had resented his busy work schedule, and had become convinced he was having affairs. When he had refused to start a family until their relationship was on a more even keel she had taken that as a sign that he regretted the marriage. The guilt she had inspired in him had taken on a haunting rawness when, after a tense exchange during a boat trip, Jasmine had stormed off in the yacht's tender, overturned on rocks and drowned.

The memory of the icy salt water dashing off rocks as he had attempted to save Jasmine started a dull ache in the scar that marred one cheekbone, a permanent reminder of that day.

Legend said Gabe's ancestor had had a positive outcome

to his passionate involvement with the woman he had married. Gabe's experience had been such that he would not allow a woman to have that kind of power over him again. As far as he was concerned, passion had its place, but only in short, controllable liaisons. Love was another thing entirely; he would not be drawn into that maelstrom again.

A rap at the door of his suite was a welcome distraction. Shrugging into a T-shirt, he opened the door to his longtime friend and Zahir's chief of security.

Xavier, who had just flown in from Zahir, strolled into the spacious lounge that adjoined Gabe's bedroom and handed him an envelope. "Special delivery."

Slitting the envelope, Gabe extracted the marriage contract he had discussed with his lawyers before leaving Zahir.

Xavier stared at the contract as if it were a bomb about to explode. "I don't believe it. You're actually going to go through with it."

Gabe headed for the state-of-the-art kitchenette that opened off the lounge. "There aren't a whole lot of options."

With the cold winds of bankruptcy at their backs and the remains of Camille's extraordinary wealth lost during the confusion of the Second World War, it was up to Gabe to restore the country's fortunes with another arranged marriage to an extremely wealthy woman.

Xavier shook his head to the offer of a glass of orange juice. "I would have thought that after Jasmine—"

"That it was time I moved on?"

Xavier's expression became impatient. "When you married Jasmine you were both too young. It's time you had a *real* marriage."

"The marriage to Jasmine was real enough." Gabe drained his glass of juice and set the glass down on the counter with a sharp click. As far as he was concerned, their marriage had been all too real. He could still feel the familiar coldness in his gut, the tightness in his chest every time he thought about the past and how completely he had failed his wife when she had needed him most. "This marriage won't be." It was prescribed and controlled, preventing any possibility of destructive, manipulative emotion. "Remember, it's a business arrangement."

Xavier, who was happily married, didn't bother to hide his incredulity. "You can't seriously think you can keep it that way. What woman will ever allow that?"

Gabe lifted a brow as he flipped to the back pages of the contract. It contained a short list of candidates and photographs of the pretty young women from wealthy families who had expressed an interest in the prestige and business opportunities inherent in a marriage to the future Sheikh of Zahir.

Xavier frowned at the list. "I still think you're making a big mistake, but I guess it's your funeral."

Gabe saw the moment Xavier realized the import of his final comment about a funeral. He cut off Xavier's apology with a curt word. They had grown up together. Xavier had been his best man when he'd gotten married, and when Jasmine had died, he had kept the press and hordes of well-meaning friends and relatives at bay, gifting Gabe the privacy he had needed. Through it all, their friendship had endured. "I have to marry at some point. Don't forget, aside from the money, Zahir needs an heir."

After Xavier left, Gabe grabbed fresh clothing and headed for the shower. He considered Xavier's comment that he and Jasmine had been too young to marry. He had been twenty, Jasmine eighteen. The marriage had lasted two years.

Flicking on the shower, he waited until steam rose off the tiles before stripping and stepping beneath the water. Now he was thirty, and as his father's only son he needed to marry and continue the family line. The prospect of a second marriage made his jaw clench. He could think of other ways to raise the money Zahir needed, Westernized ways that weren't presently a part of Zahir's constitution. But with his father recovering from cancer and wary about new investments, Gabe had accepted his father's old-fashioned solution.

Minutes later, dressed in a white shirt, red tie and dark suit, he stood drinking the dark, aromatic coffee he preferred as he stared out at the heavy rain sweeping the harbor. As cold and alien as the view was, thousands of miles from sunny Zahir, it was nevertheless familiar. Not only had his mother been born in New Zealand, but Wellington had been a home away from home for him because he had gone to school here.

Checking his watch, he placed his empty mug on the coffee table next to the marriage contract. Right now he had a breakfast meeting with both the Zahiri and New Zealand ministers for tourism. That would be followed by a string of business meetings, then a cocktail party and presentation on Zahir's attractions as a tourist destination at the consulate tonight.

Despite Gabe's resolve, he could think of better ways to spend his last day of freedom.

One more day—and night—as a bachelor, before he committed to the marriage of convenience that was his destiny.

* * *

She was destined to be loved, truly loved...

The chime of her alarm almost pulled Sarah Duval out of her dream, but the irresistible passion that held her in its grip was too singular and addictive to relinquish just yet. Eyes firmly closed against the notion of another day of unvarying routine in her teaching job, she groped for the alarm and hit the sleep button. Dragging a fluffy feather pillow over her head, she sank back into the dream.

The directness of the warrior's gaze was laden with the focused intent she had waited years to experience, as if he thought she was beautiful, or more—as if he was actually fascinated by her.

Strong fingers cupped her chin. Sarah dragged her gaze from the fascinating scar that sliced a jagged line across one taut cheekbone and clamped down on the automatic caution that gripped her, the disbelief that after years of being let down by men an outrageously attractive man could truly want her. The searing heat blasting off his bronzed torso, the rapid thud of his heart beneath her palms, didn't feel like a lie.

In point of fact, the warrior wasn't saying a lot, but Sarah was okay with that. After years of carefully studying body language, because she had learned she could not always trust what was said, she had learned to place a measure of trust in the vocabulary of the senses.

Throwing her normal no-nonsense practicality to the winds she lifted up on her toes, buried her fingers in the thick night-dark silk of his hair, and pressed herself firmly against the muscular warmth of his body. His mouth closed over hers and emotion, almost painful in its intensity, shuddered through her.

Dimly, she acknowledged that this was it. The long years of waiting were over. She would find out what it felt like to be truly wanted, to finally make love—

The shrill of the alarm once more shoved Sarah out of the dream, although the warrior's voice seemed to hang in the air, as declarative as his dark gaze.

"You are mine to hold."

An electrifying quiver ran the length of her spine, lifting all the fine hairs at her nape as she silenced the alarm. Blinking at the grayness of the morning, she registered the comforting ticking of the oil heater she'd dragged beside the bed to keep out the winter chill. She sucked in a breath in an effort to release the tension that banded her chest and the sharp, hot ache at the back of her throat. As if she really had been the focus of a powerful male's desire...

A soft thud drew her gaze to the leather-bound cover of the family journal she had been reading before she'd gone to sleep. It had slipped off the edge of her bed and fallen to the floor. The journal, which had been partially transcribed from Old French by an erudite cousin, relegated the dream to its true context—fantasy.

None of it had been real. At least no more real to Sarah than the dramatic contents of the personal diary of Camille de Vallois. A spinster and academic who had lived more than eight hundred years ago, Camille had been sold into marriage by her family. However, when her ship had foundered on the rocks of Zahir, she had made herself over as an adventurous femme fatale and gone after the man she discovered she wanted, a sheikh who had also been a battle-hardened Templar Knight. Camille had risked all for love, admittedly with the help of an enormous dowry, and she had succeeded.

Frowning, Sarah reviewed the vivid dream and reluctantly let the last remnants of the powerful emotions that had held her in thrall flicker and die. Camille's story had clearly formed the basis of the dream. Plus, the previous day, caught up in the romance she'd been reading in the journal, she had called at the Zahiri consulate and picked up a pamphlet about a scheduled exhibition of Zahiri artifacts and a lecture on their history and culture. While exiting the building in the middle of a rain shower, head down because she had forgotten her umbrella, she had run into a man so gorgeous that for long seconds her brain had refused to function.

By the time she had recovered the power of speech, he had picked up the pamphlets she'd dropped, handed them to her with a flashing grin and strode into the consulate. The hero of her dream, scar and all, had looked suspiciously like that man.

Her cheeks warmed at the memory of some of the graphic elements of the dream, the searing embrace and a toe-curling kiss that had practically melted her on the spot. It had definitely been the stuff of fantasies and nothing to do with her normal life as a staid history teacher.

In her ancestor's case, the dream had come true, but Sarah could never allow herself to forget that Camille's romance had been smoothed along by a great deal of cold hard cash. Love story or not, Sarah was willing to bet that Sheikh Kadin had known on which side his bread had been buttered.

Pushing upright in the cozy nest of her bed, she reached down and retrieved the journal, which included photocopied sheets of the original, written in Old French, plus the sections of the journal her cousin had so far transcribed.

A heavy gust hit the side of her cottage, rattling the windows and making the old kauri timbers groan. Pushing free of the heavy press of quilt and coverlet, Sarah inched her feet into fluffy slippers, belted a heavy robe around her waist and padded to the window to stare out at the stormy day.

The steep street she lived on was shrouded in gray. The sodium lamps still cast a murky glow on neatly trimmed hedges, white picket fences and the occasional wild tangle of an old rose. The houses, huddled together, cheek-by-jowl—some so close a person could barely walk between them—were neither graceful and old nor conveniently modern. Inhabited by solo homeowners like herself or young families, they were something much more useful: affordable.

Letting the drapes fall back into place, she walked to the kitchen to make herself a cup of tea before she showered and got ready for work. Her tiny kitchen, with its appliances fitted neatly to take up minimal space, was about as far away from the exotic isle of Zahir as she could get.

As she sipped hot tea, her reflection in the multipaned window over the counter bounced back at her and she found herself critically examining her appearance. With her hair bundled into a knot, her face bare of makeup, the thick robe making her look ten pounds heavier than she was, she looked washed-out, tired and…boring.

Frowning, chest tight at the thought that at twenty-eight she was no longer in the first flush of youth, she peered more closely at her reflection. Her eyes were blue; her skin was pale; her hair, when it was loose, was heavy, straight and dark. It was the faded robe that drained the color from her skin, and the tight way her hair was scraped back from her face that was so unflattering. She wasn't old.

Although she would be twenty-nine next month. In just over a year she would be thirty.

The pressurized feeling in her chest increased. She sucked in a breath, trying to ease the tension, but the thought of turning thirty made her heart hammer. She was abruptly aware of time passing, leaving her behind, of her failure to find someone special to love and who would love her back in return.

On the heels of those thoughts an old fear loomed out of the shadows. That her disastrous track record with men wasn't about bad luck or bad judgment, it was about *her*; she was the problem. Perhaps some aspect of her personality, maybe her academic bent and blunt manner, or more probably her old-fashioned insistence on being truly loved for herself before sex entered the equation, was the reason she would never be cherished by any man.

Grimly, she considered her two engagements, which had both fallen through. Her first fiancé, Roger, had gotten annoyed when she hadn't felt ready to sleep with him the week of their engagement, and so had called it off. Not a problem.

The second time she had chosen better, or so she had thought. Unfortunately, after months of dating a fellow teacher, Mark, who had seemed quite happy with her views on celibacy before marriage, she had discovered, on the morning of their wedding, that he had fallen in love with somebody else. A blonde and pretty somebody else with whom he had been sleeping for the past four months.

Normally, she didn't wallow in the painful details of those relationship mistakes. Burying her head in the sand and anaesthetizing herself with work had been a much more attractive option.

But reading the journal that had recently arrived from her cousin and dreaming that deeply sensual dream had changed her in some imperceptible way. Maybe what she was feeling was all tied up with the realization that her biological clock was ticking. Whatever the cause, she felt different this morning, tinglingly alive and acutely vulnerable, as if she were standing on the edge of a precipice.

And she knew what that precipice was: she was finally ready to try again. Her pulse sped up at the knowledge that after years of relationship limbo she wanted to love and be loved and this time, marriage or not, she wanted the passionate, heart-stopping sex. Adrenaline zinged through her veins at the thought of tossing her old relationship rulebook away. She was tired of waiting, of missing out. She wanted to take the risk, to find a man she could not just desire, but with whom she could fall recklessly, wildly in love.

A man like the dangerously handsome guy she had run into the day before.

Absently, she sipped her cooling tea. In the past, she had been black-and-white in her thinking. She had wanted all or nothing. She didn't understand how she had become that way. Maybe her deep need for emotional certainty had been fueled by the fact that her father had only ever been a sometime presence in her life. Or maybe it was because she was naturally passionate in her thinking. For most of her adult life "all or nothing" had been the catchphrase that had summed up her approach.

Whatever the cause, it had devastated her last two serious relationships and was already sounding the death knell for the lukewarm friendship she shared with an importer of antiquities and fellow history buff that was the closest thing to a romance on her dating horizon.

Her jaw firmed. If she was going to find someone to love, someone she could marry and have babies with, it was clear she would have to be more flexible than she had been in the past. She would have to change. She would have to bite the bullet and experiment with a casual affair.

And the clock was ticking.

Replacing the mug on the counter, she dragged her hair free of the elastic tie that held it in place. Feeling tense and a little shaky, she raked her fingers through the warm, heavy strands, trying to work some volume into her satin-smooth hair. With her hair tumbling loose to her waist, she looked younger and sexier. Relief made her feel ridiculously light-headed.

She dragged off the robe and let it drop to the floor. The nightie she was wearing didn't help matters. Made of cotton flannel in an unflattering shade of pale pink, it reminded her of the nightwear her grandmother used to wear. Great for cold nights, drinking hot chocolate and reading a book, but ultimately as sexy as a tent.

The only positive was that beneath the material she had a good figure. Her breasts were shapely, her waist narrow, her legs long and toned from all the walking she did.

Shivering at the chill, she dragged on the robe and returned to her bedroom. Flicking on a light, she flung her closet wide and began examining hangers of clothes she had bought for the honeymoon that hadn't happened.

Annoyed at how affected she still was by the canceled wedding and Mark's easy dismissal of her in favor of a woman who had been dishonest enough to sleep with an engaged man, she hauled out slinky clothes and dropped them on the bed. She needed to exorcise the past by either wearing the clothes as if they had not been bought for a special, life-changing occasion, or else give them away to a charity shop.

Sarah arrayed the collection of jewel-bright garments across her bed. With a start, she realized that almost four years had passed since Mark had jilted her.

Four years.

Jaw set at the time that had passed, she selected a red dress. The color was sensual and rich, the silk jersey warm to the touch. With three-quarter-length sleeves and a V-neck, the design was classic. Bought for the romantic honeymoon she had paid for in Paris then cancelled, it was also sexy and sophisticated.

Before she could change her mind, she stripped out of the robe and nightgown and pulled on the dress. The jersey settled against her skin, making her shiver. Strolling to her dressing table she examined the effect of the dress, which, worn without a bra and with her hair rumpled and loose, was startlingly sensual. The deep, rich color made her skin look creamy instead of pale, and turned her dark hair a rich shade of sable. She stared at the bold, definitely female image, feeling oddly electrified, like a sleeper waking up.

The woman in the mirror in no way looked boring or tired. She looked young and vibrant. *Available.*

Years had passed since Mark had ditched her practically at the altar. Years that she had wasted, and which had been her prime window in terms of finding a suitable mate. If she had been focused by now she would have met and married her Mr. Right, gotten pregnant and had at least one baby.

She had put her lack of success with relationships down to her heavy work schedule. According to her mother, Hannah, the real reason Sarah hadn't found a relationship was fear. Two engagements had fallen through and in her usual stubborn way Sarah had refused to go out on a limb a third time.

Hannah's solution had been to produce a constant supply of eligible men from among her interior-decorating business contacts, which was how Sarah had met Graham Southwell. Although, after several platonic dates, she had received the overwhelming impression that Graham was more interested in her connection to the missing de Vallois dowry than in an actual relationship.

As it happened she was meeting Graham that evening. After the revelation of the dream, she could not view tonight as just another dead-end date with a man who did not really see her. Tonight was an opportunity to effect the change that was already zinging through her.

She could not afford to wait any longer for her true love to find her; experience had taught her that might never happen. Like her ancestor Camille, she had to be bold. She had to formulate a plan.

By the time she was ready to leave for work she had settled on a strategy that was time-honored and uncannily close to Camille's plan to win her sheikh.

Sarah would dress to kill, and when she found the man of her dreams, she would seduce him.

Two

Sarah found a space in the parking lot next door to the historic old building that housed the Zahiri consulate. Situated just over the road from the waterfront, the entire block was dotted with grand Victorian and Edwardian buildings and a series of old warehouses that had been turned into bars and restaurants.

As she stepped out of the car, cold wind gusted in off the sea and spits of rain landed on her skin. Her hair, which she'd spent a good hour coaxing into trailing curls with a hot curling iron, swirled around her face. Turning up the collar of her coat and shivering a little, because the red silk jersey dress was not made for a cold Wellington night, she locked the car and started toward the consulate.

Feeling nervous and self-conscious about all the changes she'd made, especially her new makeup and a pair of black boots with heels a couple of inches higher than she normally wore, she hurried past a group of young men hanging around the covered area outside a bar.

The wind gusted again, making her coat flap open and lifting the flimsy skirt of her dress, revealing more leg than she was accustomed to showing. Her phone chimed as she clutched the lapels of her coat and dragged her hemline down. Ignoring a barrage of crude remarks and a piercing wolf whistle, she retrieved the phone and answered the call.

Graham had arrived early and was already inside on the off chance that he might actually get to meet the elusive Sheikh of Zahir, who was rumored to be in town. Since it was cold and on the verge of raining, he had decided not to hang around outside waiting for her as they had arranged.

Irritated but unsurprised by Graham's lack of consideration, Sarah walked up the steps to the consulate and strolled into the foyer, which was well lit and warm.

She was greeted by a burly man with a shaved head who was dressed in a beautifully cut suit. He checked her invitation and noted her name on a register. When he handed the invitation back, his gaze was piercing. In New Zealand it was unusual to be scrutinized so thoroughly. She was almost certain he wasn't just a consulate official. With the sheikh in residence it was more likely that the man was one of the sheikh's bodyguards. Though a Christian nation, Zahir, a Mediterranean island, was caught between the Middle East and Europe. The elderly sheikh had been kidnapped some years ago and so now was rumored to always travel with an armed escort.

She hung her coat on the rack provided. Ignoring an

attack of nerves caused by losing the cozy, protective outer layer that had mostly hidden the red dress, she walked through an elegant hallway and into a crowded reception room. It was a cocktail party and promotional evening aimed at selling Zahir, with its colorful history as a Templar outpost, as a tourist destination. Sarah had expected little black dresses and the rich exotic colors of the East to abound, but crisp business suits and black and gray dresses toned down by jackets created a subdued monochrome against which she stood out like an overbright bird of paradise.

Sarah's stomach sank. When she had read the pamphlet she hadn't seen the evening as focused on business, but if she didn't miss her guess, most of the guests were business types, probably tour operators and travel agents and no doubt a smattering of government officials.

Deciding to brazen it out, she moved to a display concerning the mysterious disappearance of the remains of Camille's dowry. Hidden by a member of the sheikh's family at the time of the evacuation during the Second World War, the location of the hiding place had been lost when the family member died in a bombing raid.

A short, balding man in a gray suit also stopped by the display, but seemed more mesmerized by the faint shadowy hollow of her cleavage. Annoyed by his rudeness, she sent him the kind of quelling glance that would have had her pupils scrambling to apply themselves to their study. As he scuttled away, she thought longingly about retrieving her coat and covering up the alluring brightness of the dress, but she refused to cut and run because she was attracting male attention. After all, that had been the whole point.

A waiter offered her a glass of wine. A little desper-

ately, she took a glass and sipped slowly as she moved
to a display of Templar weaponry. Instantly riveted by a
history she found even more fascinating after immersing
herself in Camille's journal, Sarah read the notes about
the Templar band under the command of Sheikh Kadin.
Setting her glass down on a nearby table, she stepped
closer, irresistibly drawn to the largest weapon—a grim,
pitted sword that had clearly seen hard use. A small label
indicated the sword had belonged to the sheikh. In that
moment she remembered a passage of the journal, which
had outlined Camille's first meeting with Kadin.

*"An overlarge warrior with a black, soaked mane,
dark eyes narrowed against the wind, a workmanlike
blade gripped in his battle-scarred hand."*

The fascination that had gripped Sarah as she'd read
Camille's account came back full force. A small sign
warned against touching the displays, but the powerful
compulsion to immerse herself in sensation, to touch the
sword, far outweighed the officious red wording.

Breath held, her fingertips brushed the gleaming
grip where the chasing etched into the bronze was worn
smooth by use. The chill of the metal struck through her
skin. A split second later, the bracket holding the sword
came loose and the heavy weapon toppled, hitting the
carpeted floor with a thud.

Mortified, Sarah reached for the sword, hoping to
prop it against the display before anyone noticed. Before
she could grab it, a large tanned hand closed around the
bronze grip. With fluid grace, a tall, broad-shouldered
man straightened, the blade in his hand, and her heart
slammed once, hard, as her dream world and the present fused.

The warrior.

That seemed the only adequate description. The man was tall enough that her gaze was firmly centered on his jaw. Heart pounding, she tilted her head and stared directly into the amber gleam of eyes that, for a split second, she fully expected to be as passionately focused on her as those of the warrior who had haunted her dream.

Her breath caught in the back of her throat as she recognized the man she had run into the previous day. The curious tension that had invested the dream drew every muscle taut as she took in black hair cut crisp and short, the blade-straight nose and the intriguing scar on his cheekbone. The planes and angles of his face were mouthwateringly clean-cut, although any sense of perfection was lost in the grim line of his jaw and the lash of the scar.

His brows drew together as if he recognized her and was trying to remember from exactly where. A split second later his gaze shuttered and she had to wonder if she'd imagined that moment of intense interest.

Or, on a more practical note, if he was married. As a single woman with years of dating experience, it would not be the first time she had been checked out by a man who then suddenly recalled that he was committed elsewhere.

His gaze dropped to her hands. "Are you all right? For a moment, I thought you might have cut yourself."

The low, rough timbre of his voice, the cosmopolitan accent, was definitely European, but with a slow cadence that indicated he had spent time in the States. The accent, along with the short cut of his hair and the suit, added to the impression that had been forming, the only one that made sense—he was either an aide to the sheikh or a bodyguard. Given his muscular build, and the fact that he had arrived within seconds of her touching the sword, she would go with the security option.

She dredged up a smile and displayed her palms to show she wasn't injured. "I'm fine, just a little startled the sword wasn't secured. Especially since it belonged to Sheikh Kadin."

For another heart-pounding moment his gaze seemed riveted on her mouth. "You're right, the Wolf of Zahir would not have been so careless. I'll have a word with the staff who set up the display."

She dragged her gaze from the line of his jaw. "Oh no, really…it was completely my fault. I shouldn't have touched the sword." Shouldn't have allowed herself to be distracted by her ancestor's passionate love story when she needed to apply herself to establishing her own.

With an easy movement, he propped the weapon against the display board. As he did so an angled spotlight above gleamed over his damaged cheekbone, and cast a shadow over the inky curve of his lashes. Suddenly the dream warrior, as riveting as he had been, seemed too cosmetically perfect and lacking in personality. From memory, he had also been oddly compliant. In the way of dreams, he had done exactly what she had wanted, in contrast to this man who looked as seasoned and uncompromising as the Templar Knight who had originally wielded the sword.

To her surprise, instead of moving on, he held out his hand and introduced himself as Gabriel, Gabe for short.

Surprised at the informality and that he seemed to want to keep the conversation going, Sarah briefly gripped his hand as she supplied her name. Tingling warmth shot through her at the rough heat of his palm. "I'm a history teacher."

She caught the flash of surprise in his expression and her mood dropped like a stone. He was tall, gorgeous, *hot*—as different from Graham as a dark lion from a tabby cat. Incredibly, he also seemed to be interested in her, and she had just ruined the outward impression of sexy sophistication she'd spent hours creating. If she'd had her wits about her she would have relegated her teaching occupation to some dusty dark hole and claimed an interest in travelling to exotic places.

"I'm guessing since you're at the exhibition that it's Templar history?"

Her mood dropped even further when she realized she now had to tell him how boring and prosaic her subjects were. "I specialize in the industrial revolution and the First and Second World Wars." She let out a resigned breath, convinced they had nothing in common. "What about you?"

"Five years at Harvard. It was useful."

Hope flared anew. "Harvard. That sounds like law, or business."

"Business, I'm afraid."

He sounded almost as apologetic as she had been. Her heart beat faster. Not a bodyguard then, despite the muscle. Perhaps he was one of the sheikh's financial advisors. She was riveted by the thought that maybe all wasn't lost.

Just as she was searching for some small talk, two Arabic men in suits joined them. The taller one, carrying a screwdriver, immediately set about refixing the bracket that had held the sword. The other suit, a plump man with a tag that proclaimed he was Tarik ben Abdel, the consulate administration manager, sent her a disapproving glance. He then button-holed Gabe and launched into a tirade in a liquid tongue she recognized as Zahiri.

Gabe cut him off with a flat, soft phrase, although Sarah was distracted from the exchange. Graham had appeared just yards away, head swiveling as if he had finally remembered to search for her. His gaze passed over her then shot back to linger on the hint of cleavage at the V of her dress. When he fished in his pocket for his cell phone and turned away, an irritated look on his face, she realized that, aside from checking out her chest, he had failed to recognize her.

Tarik, with a last disapproving glance at her, marched away, the second suit trailing behind. She noticed that the sword was once again affixed to the display.

Sarah was suddenly blazingly aware that the tall dark man hadn't left as she had expected him to and that he was studying her with an enigmatic expression, as if he'd logged the exchange with Graham.

Still mortified at the fuss she'd created, she rushed to apologize. "I read the sign. I know I shouldn't have touched the sword, that artifacts can be vulnerable to skin oils and salts—"

"Tarik wasn't worried that the sword might be damaged. It survived the Third Crusade, so a fall onto soft carpet is hardly likely to cause harm. He was more concerned about the tradition that goes with the sword."

Understanding dawned. If there had been a preeminent symbol of manhood in the Middle Ages, it had been the sword, and this had been a Templar sword. "Of course, the Templar vow of chastity."

Amusement gleamed in his gaze. "And a superstition that a woman's touch would somehow disable a warrior's potency in battle."

A curious warmth hummed through her as she realized that, as nerve-racking as the exchange had started out, she was actually enjoying talking to the most dangerously attractive man she had ever met. "Sounds more like a convenient way of shifting blame for a lackluster performance on the battlefield."

"Possibly." Gabe's mouth kicked up at one corner, softening the line of his jaw and revealing the slightest hint of an indentation. "But, back then, on Zahir, if a woman handled a man's sword, it was also viewed as a declaration of intent."

Breath held, Sarah found herself waiting for the dimple to be more fully realized. "What if she was simply curious?"

His gaze locked with hers and a tension far more acute than any she had experienced in her dream flared to life. "Then the warrior might demand a forfeit. Although most of the Templars that landed on Zahir eventually gave up their vows."

"Including the sheikh, who married."

The cooling of his expression as she mentioned marriage was like a dash of cold water. For the second time she wondered if he was married. Disappointment cascaded through her at the thought. A glance at his left hand confirmed there was no ring, although that meant nothing. He could be married, with children, and never wear a ring.

A faint buzz emanated from his jacket pocket. With a frown that sent a dart of pleasure through her, because it conveyed that he didn't want to be interrupted, he excused himself and half turned away to take the call.

Unsettled and on edge because she was clearly developing an unhealthy fascination for a complete stranger,

Sarah remembered her glass of wine. As she took a steadying sip, her cell phone chimed. Setting the glass back down, she rummaged in her handbag and found the phone and another text from Graham. Although there was nothing romantic or even polite about the words. Where are you?

Annoyed at his blunt irritation, the cavalier way he hadn't bothered to meet her as they had arranged, Sarah punched the delete key. She might be a victim of the love game, but she would not be a doormat. Temper on a slow simmer, she shoved the phone back in her handbag.

Gabe terminated his call. "Are you with someone? I noticed you came in alone."

Suddenly the tension was thick enough to cut, although she couldn't invest the knowledge that he had noticed her entrance with too much importance. She was the only person dressed in red in a sea of black and gray; of course he had noticed her. "Uh, I was supposed to meet someone..."

"A man."

She crushed the urge to say she wasn't meeting another man; that would have been a lie. "Yes."

He nodded, his expression remote, but she was left with the unmistakable impression that if she had said she was alone the evening might have taken a more exciting turn than she could ever expect with Graham.

His expression suddenly neutral, Gabe checked his watch. "If you'll excuse me. I have a call to make."

Sarah squashed a plunging sense of disappointment. As he walked away, she forced herself to look around for Graham.

She spotted him across the room involved in an animated discussion with a man wearing a business suit and a kaffiyeh, the traditional Arabic headdress. She studied the Arab man, who she assumed must be the sheikh. She had read a lot about Zahir, but most of it had been history, since Zahir was a small, peaceful country that didn't normally make the news. She knew that the sheikh was on the elderly side, and that he had married a New Zealander, a woman who had originally come from Wellington, which explained Zahir's close ties with her country.

She strolled closer just as the man with the kaffiyeh moved away and finally managed to make eye contact with Graham.

The blankness of his expression changed to incredulity. *"You."*

Not for the first time Sarah looked at Graham and wondered how such a pleasantly handsome man could inspire little more in her than annoyance. "That's right, your date."

He shook his head as if he couldn't quite believe what he was seeing. "If you'd told me you were going to change your appearance—"

Her jaw locked at Graham's unflattering response, as if the act of putting on a dress, a little extra makeup and messing with her hair was some kind of disguise. "This *is* how I look."

He stared at her mouth, making her wonder if she'd been a little too heavy on the berry lip gloss. "Not usually. If you had, we might have hit it off a little better."

Sarah realized there was one very good reason she had never been able to really like Graham. Not only was he self-centered with a roving eye, he had a nasty streak. She had been looking for a prince and, as usual, had ended up dating a frog. "How about I make it easy for us both. From now on don't call and don't come around to my mother's house for dinner. A clean break would suit me."

His expression took on a shifty cast. "What about the journal? You said I could look at it."

"That was all you really wanted, wasn't it?"

"I wouldn't say that, exactly."

No, because what he really wanted was to find the lost dowry and cash in on it. Sarah drew a deep breath and let it out slowly. The first two men in her life had dumped her for other women; that she could accept. Graham preferring *a book* and the possibility of cold hard cash over her was the proverbial last straw. "Forget the journal. It's a private, family document. Hell would freeze solid before I'd give it to you."

Feeling angry and hurt, hating the fact that she had lost her temper but relieved she had finally finished with Graham, Sarah spun on her heel then froze as she spotted Gabe talking with an elderly lady. He was close enough that he had probably heard some of her conversation with Graham. His gaze locked with hers, sharp and uncomplicatedly male, and for a moment the room full of people ceased to exist. Then a waiter strolled past with a tray filled with glasses, breaking the spell.

Her stomach clenched on a sharp jab of feminine intuition, that despite knowing she had a date, after he had made his call, Gabe had come looking for her. When he'd seen her talking with Graham, he'd stopped far enough away to allow her privacy—*to allow her a choice*—but close enough to keep an eye on her.

Graham didn't find her attractive, but she was suddenly acutely aware that Gabe did. Talking to him at the sword display had been easy; there had been nothing at stake. Instinctively, she knew a second conversation meant a whole lot more. It meant she would have to make a decision. Suddenly the whole concept of abandoning her rule about no sex before commitment seemed full of holes when what she really wanted was love, not sex.

Feeling utterly out of her depth, her chest tight, she dragged her gaze away and made a beeline for the ladies' room and the chance to regroup.

Pushing the door open, she stepped into a pretty tiled bathroom. Her reflection bounced back at her, tousled hair and smoky eyes, sleek dress and black boots. Her cheeks flushed as she registered what Gabe was seeing. Graham was right. *She* barely recognized herself. The woman who stared back at her looked exotic and assured. Experienced.

She wondered if all Gabe saw was the outer package and the possibility of a night of no-strings passion. What if, like Graham, Gabe wouldn't be attracted to who she really was?

She found her lipstick and reapplied it, her fingers shaking very slightly. The knowledge that Gabe was attracted to her, that the improvement she had made to her appearance had worked, was unsettling. She hadn't expected such an instant response.

She should be buoyed by her success. Instead, she felt on edge and, for want of a better word, vulnerable. Maybe it was because in her mind Gabe had become linked with the dream that had been the catalyst for all of this change. She knew almost nothing about him, but in the moment he had picked up the sword, he had made an indelible impression; he had symbolized what she wanted.

She stopped dead as the final piece of the puzzle of

her dysfunction with men dropped neatly into place. She
drew a deep breath. She felt like quietly banging her head
against the nearest wall, but that would not be a good
idea with all the security personnel roaming around.
The reason she had not been intimate with anyone, even
her fiancés, was because, hidden beneath the logic and
practicality and years of academia, she was an idealist.
Worse, she was a *romantic*.

Maybe all the years of burying her head in history
books had changed her in some fundamental way because it was now blindingly clear why an ordinary, ev-
eryday kind of guy with a nine-to-five job had never
been quite enough. Somehow, despite common sense,
in her heart of hearts, she had wanted the kind of seasoned, bedrock strength and stirring romanticism that it
was difficult to find in the twenty-first century.

She had wanted a knight.

When she stepped back into the reception room, despite giving herself a good talking-to about the dan-
gers of projecting crazy romantic fantasies onto a man
she barely knew, she found herself instantly looking
for Gabe. When she couldn't find him, disappointment
gripped her. In an adjacent room the lecture on Zahir was
beginning. She strolled inside and saw him at the back,
in conversation with a well-known government official.

The jolt in her stomach, the relief and the tingling
heat that flooded her, should have been warning enough.
In the space of an hour she had somehow fallen into a
heady infatuation with a virtual stranger, but after years
of emotional limbo the blood racing through her veins,
the crazy cocktail of emotions, was addictive. Just as she
debated what to do—brazenly approach Gabe or wimp
out completely and ignore the intense emotions—an el-

egant young woman walked up to Gabe and flung her arms around him.

Numb with disappointment, Sarah turned on her heel, walked into the foyer and began searching for her coat. She was fiercely glad she hadn't approached Gabe, because he appeared to have a girlfriend, or, more probably, a wife.

Frowning, she flipped through the rack of coats again and pulled out a coat which looked like hers, but which wasn't. Someone had obviously left in a hurry and taken her coat by mistake. As much as she needed a coat, she drew the line at helping herself to one she knew wasn't hers. Besides, she still had her small telescopic umbrella, which fit in her handbag. In the wind, it probably wouldn't last long, but it was better than nothing.

Outside, lightning flickered and, in the distance, thunder crashed. As Murphy's Law would have it, the rain, which had been light earlier was now tropical.

Extracting the umbrella, Sarah paused by the antique double doors of the entrance, reluctant to step out into such a heavy downpour. A flicker of movement turned her head. She saw Gabe speaking to the tall, bald man who had checked her invitation.

Aware that in just a few seconds he could turn and see her standing in the foyer, watching him, she pushed open the doors and stepped outside.

As she descended the steps the wind, damp with rain and bitingly cold, sent a raw shiver through her. She came to a halt at the edge of the sheltered area. Flipping up her umbrella, she stepped into the wet and wild night.

The bottom half of her dress was almost instantly soaked. Water seeped into the soles of her boots as she threaded through cars that gleamed beneath streetlights.

The parking lot seemed farther away than when she had arrived. In the murky darkness, the garish lights from the nightclub were overbright, although the steady thud of music was now muted by the sound of the rain.

Dragging soaked hair from her eyes and glad she was wearing waterproof mascara, she fumbled in her bag, searching for keys. She depressed the key lock, suddenly wishing she hadn't parked quite so close to the nightclub. The lights of her car flashed and she headed for the welcome beacon of her small hatchback. As she opened the door, she became aware of a cluster of dark shadows congregated beneath the overhang of the warehouse-size building that housed the nightclub. Slamming the door closed, she immediately locked it, just in case the youths tried something silly.

She inserted her key into the ignition. The starter motor made its familiar high-pitched whine, but the motor itself refused to fire. Feeling a little desperate, she tried again, then a third time. When the starter took on a deeper, slower sound, as if the battery was becoming drained, she immediately stopped. She was no mechanic but, at a guess, the wind had driven rain under the hood and the electronics had gotten wet. The car wouldn't start until she managed to dry the motor. If she kept using the starter she would also end up with a flat battery.

She considered ringing her mother then immediately dismissed the thought. Hannah was overseas on a buying trip for her interior-decorating business. Graham was still inside. As much as she didn't want to ask him, he would have to help her. Groaning, she tried texting. When minutes passed with no reply, she bit the bullet and rang him. The call went through to voice mail.

Deciding that it would be a whole lot simpler to just walk back into the consulate to get help, Sarah grabbed her bag and stepped out into the rain, which had thankfully eased to a fine drizzle. A tap on her shoulder made her start.

"Having trouble, darlin'?"

She stiffened at the shock of being touched by a stranger and stepped away from the powerful whiff of alcohol fumes. "Nothing I can't handle, thanks."

He grinned hazily. "I'd sure like to help you."

There was a stifled laugh somewhere behind him. With a jolt Sarah realized they had been joined by two more men, both of them like the first, darkly dressed, wearing leather and decorated with tattoos and multiple piercings.

The taller of the two grinned. "Don't keep her to yourself, Ty. We'd *all* like to help the lady."

Jaw set, Sarah debated trying to get back into the car and locking the doors, but decided against that. If she did, they could prevent her from closing the door and before she knew where she was, they would be inside the car with her and she would be in a worse position.

Rape. The horrifying thought shuddered through her. She was a virgin. She had saved herself for love and marriage. The first time she was with a man could not be because she was being forced.

Footsteps sounded across the parking lot. They were no longer alone. Thinking quickly, Sarah's fingers tightened on her umbrella. It wasn't much of a weapon, but she would use it if she had to. "I don't need help. My boyfriend's here. He'll fix the car."

"What boyfriend?" The taller man grabbed her arm as she edged away.

Jaw gritted, Sara brought the umbrella's wooden handle crashing down on the man's fingers.

"This one," a dark voice murmured, as Gabe stepped around a chunky utility vehicle into the light.

Three

Rubbing bruised knuckles, the tall guy, who now didn't seem large at all compared to Gabe, stumbled backward. "Hey, sorry, man," he mumbled. "Didn't know she was taken."

Gabe glided closer. When he stretched out his hand, it seemed the most natural thing in the world to put her fingers in his. "Even if she wasn't 'taken' you shouldn't have gone near her. But, as you said, she is taken, so don't bother her again."

Tall Guy took another step backward. The other two had already climbed into a car decorated with dents. He held one hand up in a placating gesture as he fumbled open the rear passenger door. "Yeah, man. She's yours. Totally. We won't bother her again."

He clambered into the car, which jolted into motion with a squeal of tires.

Gabe released his grip on her hand. "Are you okay?"

Sarah replaced her car keys in her bag. She was cold and her fingers were shaking, but she barely noticed because she was so focused on the fact that Gabe had come after her. She didn't know how he had located her in the dark, or why he had walked out into the rain to find her, just that he had. "I am now, thank you."

"Problem with your car?"

She blinked at the shift of topic. His gaze was still fixed on the taillights of the retreating car. The steely remoteness of his expression sent a chill down her spine. He looked more than capable of backing his flatly delivered challenge with physical force.

A fierce, oddly primitive sense of satisfaction curled through her. Gabe had not only come to her aid, but he had been prepared to physically fight for her.

When he repeated the question about the car, she realized he was deliberately distracting her from the nastiness of the encounter. Suppressing a shiver, she replaced her umbrella in her bag. "I think the electronics got wet."

Gabe, who had walked around to the front of her car, took a sleek phone out of his pocket and stabbed a short dial. "Is there still a charge in the battery?"

"I stopped before it went flat."

"Good." Gabe spoke quietly into his phone in the same liquid Zahiri she had heard him use before then slipped the cell back in his jacket pocket. "Xavier will have a look at the car. He's not a mechanic, but he spends a lot of his spare time tinkering with cars."

She hooked the strap of her bag more securely over her shoulder. It was an odd moment to register that the wind had dropped, leaving an eerie calm after the storm. With mist rising off the wet concrete, wreathing the cars and forming a halo around the street lamps, the night now seemed peaceful.

With a reflexive shiver she rubbed at her chilled arms and tried not to let her teeth chatter. Now that she was no longer buzzing with adrenaline the cold seemed to be seeping into her bones. "I suppose Xavier is one of the sheikh's bodyguards." The remark was shamelessly probing but she didn't care. She suddenly needed to know more about Gabe, what he did for a living, how long he would be in Wellington, when or *if* he was coming back—

His gaze glittered over her, making her aware of the soaked red dress clinging to her skin, her hair trailing wetly around her cheeks. "Only when the sheikh leaves Zahir."

The answer was confusing, as if the sheikh was still in Zahir when Sarah knew him to be here, in Wellington. But with Gabe walking toward her, dark trousers clinging low on narrow hips, his jacket damply molded to broad shoulders, white shirt plastered to his chest so that the bronze of his skin glowed through, it was hard to concentrate on unraveling subtleties.

He frowned. "You're cold. Have you got a coat in the car?"

"No c-coat. Someone at the consulate took mine by mistake."

A moment later, his jacket dropped around her shoulders, swamping her with warmth and filling her nostrils with the scent of clean male and an enticing hint of sandalwood. An electrifying thrill shot through her, reminding her of the sharp, visceral jolt she had felt when Gabe had said she was his.

He was briefly close enough that she felt the heat radiating off his body, and she had to resist the urge to sway a few inches closer to that delicious warmth. Her fingers closed on the fine weave of the jacket lapels, hugging the fabric closer. Despite everything, all of the warnings she was giving herself, she couldn't help loving that she was wearing his jacket, which was so large the sleeves dropped almost to her knees. After the nasty scenes with Graham and the leather-clad thugs, Gabe's chivalry—his consideration, as if she truly mattered to him—was a soothing balm.

Gabe checked his watch. "Xavier's on his way. If you'll give me your car keys, he'll take a look. In the meantime I suggest you come with me back to the consulate. There's a guest suite there, so you can dry off while you wait."

A vivid flash of the young woman flinging her arms around him made Sarah stiffen. "Won't your...girlfriend mind?"

His expression registered his surprise at the question. "I don't have a girlfriend. If you're referring to the young woman who came into the lecture, she was a cousin I haven't seen in years. She dropped in because she knew I was leaving in the morning."

The relief that the pretty girl wasn't a love interest was almost instantly replaced by the depressing confirmation that Gabe was leaving in a matter of hours.

His hand briefly cupped her elbow as he helped her step up onto the higher level of the consulate parking lot. "Is she the reason you left the lecture?"

Her mouth went dry at the bluntness of the question but after everything that had happened, somehow it didn't seem as intrusive as it should have been. It would have been easy to say she'd had a fight with Graham and was upset, but the truth was, whatever she had felt for Graham had been utterly overshadowed by her response to Gabe.

He was leaving in just a few hours.

Lifting her chin, she met his gaze. There was no point trying to hide what was already clear to him. She had been hurt and disappointed when she had thought he was committed to another woman. "Yes."

There was a moment of vibrating silence, filled by the muted sound of their footfalls on wet pavement, the distant wash of the sea and the slow drip of water splashing off a gutter. Sarah's stomach tightened as Gabe directed her to a door at the side of the consulate building and held it for her. Somehow, in the space of a little over an hour they had achieved a level of intimacy that made her stomach tighten and her pulse pound. But her time alone with him was almost up. Soon they would be joined by other people and a conversation that had become unexpectedly important would be over.

As if to underscore her thoughts, the plump administrative official, Tarik, strode down the corridor toward them, disapproval pulling his brows into a dark line. She drew a breath, but it was already too late to ask Gabe the question that was burning inside her.

He knew she was strongly attracted to him and that was why she had left the consulate so quickly. But was attraction the reason he had come looking for her?

Gabe left Sarah freshening up in the guest room that opened onto his study and strode along the hall to his suite. The moment he had seen the thug lay hands on her replayed through his mind, making him tense. When he had registered the danger, the half-formed desires and intentions that had driven him out into the stormy night had coalesced into one burning reality.

He wanted Sarah Duval.

He hadn't liked the fact that she'd had a date. He had liked it even less that the drunk thought he could simply reach out and touch her. Crazily, because Gabe barely knew her and had no interest in emotional attachments, his attraction to Sarah had coalesced into the kind of knee-jerk possessiveness he could not afford on the eve of his engagement. But, as hard as he tried to shake it, he couldn't—for one simple reason. In his mind he had already claimed her.

As he unlocked the door, Xavier stepped out of the elevator and followed Gabe into the suite. Gabe grabbed a towel from the bathroom and began blotting his hair and face. "What's the verdict on the car?"

Xavier shrugged. "We could have it going in half an hour if we put it in the consulate garage, but to get it there we'll need to tow it and none of the hire vehicles have tow bars. The best-case scenario is that I call her a taxi."

"No." Gabe unknotted his tie and peeled out of his wet shirt and tossed both in the laundry basket.

The sensible thing was to do what Xavier suggested. The last thing he needed was a complication that would make the commitment he had to make in the morning even more difficult. But ever since Sarah had walked into the reception room, glowing like a fiery beacon in red, her dark hair a sexy tousled mass, the obligation and duty of his impending marriage had seemed secondary. When she had disobeyed all instructions and laid her hand on his ancestor's sword, he had been entranced.

Somehow, the fact that she had knocked the sword,

which was practically a sacred object on Zahir, off its bracket had only made her more interesting.

She was a *history* teacher. Against all odds, he found himself grinning.

Like no history teacher he'd ever seen.

Gabe strolled into his bedroom to find a clean shirt. In the past hour something curious had happened. He felt lighter and more carefree, as if a weight had lifted off him.

Because for the first time in years when he had looked at another woman, he hadn't been haunted by thoughts of Jasmine.

He guessed the fact that Sarah was literally Jasmine's polar opposite—tall and curvy with a steady, resolute gaze and hints of a fiery temper, instead of tiny and fragile and sweetly feminine—had helped. When Sarah had toppled Kadin's sword, in some odd way the separation from his past had seemed complete. Jasmine had hated all of the old Templar relics and the violent history that went with them. Sarah had seemed fascinated. From the way she had wielded her umbrella in the parking lot, he was willing to bet she would not be averse to holding a sword.

He stared at his crisply starched shirts in the closet, looking for something that didn't belong in a boardroom. Clothing that might indicate that he had a life. "I'm taking her home."

Xavier muttered something soft and short. "I don't think that's a good idea. Neither will your father."

Gabe shrugged into a dark shirt and buttoned it. The searing attraction that had sent him walking out into the night to find Sarah settled into grim determination. Xavier's unease mirrored his own because it was a fact that Gabe didn't want to just spend time with Sarah—he wanted her. Period. But just hours out from signing his life away, he was in no mood to deny a response he thought he would never feel again. "Right now a whole lot of things are happening that are not exactly good ideas."

An outmoded financial system that did not allow for the foreign investment Gabe had been advocating for years, and the marriage that *was* Zahir's financial rescue plan.

"The marriage is just an arrangement, you could have an—"

"No." Zahir was Western, but it was also extremely conservative. And Gabe was clear on one fact: once he was married he would not dishonor his vows or his family's integrity.

Xavier looked uncomfortable. "Sometimes I forget the pressure you're under. But what do you know about this woman? She could be some hard-nosed journalist angling for a story."

"Sarah's not a journalist." Gabe shrugged into a soft black leather jacket. "And she won't go to the press."

"You can't know that. You've only just met her. You have no idea what she'll do."

Gabe went still inside as a memory flickered. Cold rain scything, a dark-haired woman, head down against the weather, stepping around a corner. As his hands had shot out to stop her caroming into him he had noticed that her hair had been scraped back and her face had been almost bare of makeup. *She* had looked like a history teacher. But it had been Sarah, her eyes that deep, pure blue, the faintly imperious nose and exquisite cheekbones, the soft, generous mouth.

Instead of tempering his attraction, the recollection had the disconcerting effect of deepening it. In that moment, Gabe recognized the quality that drew him to Sarah most of all—the fact that in the midst of all the superficiality of the social world he usually moved in she was exactly what she seemed, a refreshingly direct woman unafraid to reach out and take what she wanted. "I met her yesterday."

Xavier's brows jerked together. "That makes it even worse."

Everything Xavier was saying was true. Normally he didn't pursue women he had only just met. Because of his position, he accepted that security checks on the women he dated were a fact of life. But ever since he had woken up that morning he had been restless and in no mood to be controlled. "Relax. She doesn't know who I am."

"How is that possible?"

"I think she expected my father to be here." Gabe walked through to the sitting room and pointedly held the door for Xavier. "I don't need an escort. As of now you're off duty. Take the rest of the night off."

Gabe waited until Xavier disappeared into the elevator before walking down the corridor to check on Sarah's progress in the guest suite. He could hear the sound of the hair dryer in the bathroom, so he returned to his suite to check his laptop. There was a message from his father and one from their lawyer, Hadad. Both messages, naturally, were centered on the contract Xavier had delivered.

He replied briefly to both then, jaw set, sat down to examine the list of marriage candidates that was clipped to the back of the contract. The candidate his parents preferred was at the top of the list.

He studied the color photo of Nadia Fortier. She was

slim and beautifully dressed, with long dark hair. She had to be all of eighteen.

He checked the basic information that had been provided. He saw he had been wrong about Nadia's age; she was twenty, a whole two years older than he had thought. And a good ten years his junior.

He flipped through the rest of the candidates. There were four in all. Extremely wealthy and young, all from good families, most of them with either noble or royal connections. Girls straight from exclusive finishing schools, groomed to make very good marriages as their designated career paths.

His gaze snagged on another notation: "guaranteed pure."

His jaw tensed. He realized that the situation was probably even more stressful for the girls, but he was beginning to feel like a prize stallion being led to stud. Broodingly, he wondered what kind of description of him they had received.

Tossing the document down on the coffee table, he strolled to one of the tall sash windows that looked out over the city streets. On a personal level he would not have dated any one of those candidates purely on the grounds that they were too young. He doubted they had any interests in common on which to build a marriage. The notation about purity explained the emphasis on youth, but as perfect and beautiful as each one was, none of them inspired even the remotest flicker of desire.

Unlike Sarah.

In that moment, the urge to do the unthinkable, to bail out of the arranged marriage and immerse himself in a tangled, messy, flamboyant affair with the very interesting Ms. Duval was irresistibly, powerfully appealing.

Massaging the taut muscles at his nape, he strode into his bedroom and found the keys to the Jeep that had been rented for him while he was in New Zealand. As he did so, his gaze snagged on the portrait of Kadin and Camille. Camille was dressed in flamboyant red, her dark gaze composed and direct, and for a split second he had an inkling of the fascination that had dominated his ancestor's life. The thought was like a dash of cold water. It was an obsession Gabe was determined would not dominate him.

He had already had a taste of the manipulation that went hand in hand with emotional excess. As tempting as it would be to toss tradition and his country's need and do exactly what he wanted, he could not walk away from his responsibilities.

Exiting the suite, he walked back to the guest room, his mood once again remote. He could understand Xavier's anxiety, because Gabe's behavior was distinctly out of character. Normally he took responsibility and did the right thing, and tomorrow he would choose which candidate he would marry. He had given his word.

But right now, tonight, he didn't want to think about the future. He was determined to accept the invitation he had seen in Sarah's eyes.

He was going to spend his last few hours of freedom with his quirky, fascinating lady in red.

Sarah finished blow-drying her hair and stared at the result in the gilt-framed mirror that dominated the ivory marble bathroom. With its gold taps and step-down bath, the room was utterly decadent. Her makeup was gone, washed off in the rain, and her hair had lost all of its curl. It fell in a shiny but depressingly straight waterfall to her waist. Her dress was still damp and clinging to her skin, but thankfully the silk seemed to be drying fast.

With all the glamor and magic of the makeover gone, there was no getting past the fact that, like Cinderella at the stroke of midnight, she was once again plain-Jane Sarah Duval. Although, she no longer felt like a plain-Jane. Her cheeks were softly flushed, and her eyes had a depth and sparkle she had never noticed.

Maybe that was because, just when she had thought there was no chance with Gabe, he had walked out of the night and rescued her. Now, she had been admitted to the hushed elegance of one of the sheikh's private apartments and suddenly the scenario she had planned seemed terrifyingly possible.

Placing the fluffy oversize towel she'd used in a laundry hamper, she checked that she hadn't left anything behind, hooked the strap of her bag over her shoulder and walked out into the luxuriously furnished bedroom, which opened onto a study.

Her heart slammed hard in her chest when she spotted Gabe standing at one of the tall sash windows in the study, watching the rain, which was once again pounding down. As he turned, she caught the flare of appreciation in his gaze and at the same time noticed that he had changed into dry clothes. If he'd looked formidable and just a little remote in a suit, the dark, soft shirt and black leather jacket, narrow trousers and black boots achieved the exact opposite, making him look younger and infinitely more approachable.

He indicated the rain streaming down the window. "With this weather, there's nothing we can do about the car tonight. If you want a lift home I can drop you. Or if you'd prefer I'll call a taxi."

Her heart sped up at the offer. The sensible thing, of course, would be to call a taxi but the instant she considered that option, she knew she wasn't going to take it. "If you could drop me, I'd appreciate it."

"No problem." Gabe picked up a set of keys he must have placed on a side table.

As he opened the door, she noticed an oil painting of a man dressed in robes on the wall. "Is that the sheikh?"

He glanced at the painting, but didn't seem inclined to linger. "Yes."

The painting had obviously been done when the sheikh was a lot younger, but even so, with his clipped beard and wearing traditional robes, it was difficult to see exactly what he looked like. He didn't look a lot like the man Graham had been talking to at the reception, but with the facial hair it was hard to tell. "Are there any paintings of Sheikh Kadin?"

Gabe went very still as he held the door for her. "The first Sheikh Kadin?"

She stepped out into the corridor, distracted by the sudden curtness of his tone. "I didn't realize there was more than one."

Gabe pressed a button on a sleek, private elevator and gestured that she precede him. "The name reoccurs practically every second generation in the sheikh's family." He pressed the button for the ground floor. "The name is also popular on Zahir, mostly because it's linked with prosperity."

She frowned at the flatness of his tone. "You don't sound overly impressed by the first sheikh."

"It's ancient history."

"And an ancient love story."

The doors slid open. Gabe waited for her to exit first. "According to tradition."

Her head came up at the implication. "You don't think love was involved?"

Gabe indicated a gleaming Jeep Cherokee situated at the far end of the cavernous garage, next to the doors. "Kadin was broke, Camille was wealthy. What are the odds?"

Even though she had entertained similar thoughts about Kadin's motives, she frowned as they strolled through the dim shadows. After reading Camille's very personal revelations about how strongly she had been attracted to Kadin, she couldn't help taking his comments personally. "So I suppose you think that just because Kadin was a knight and good-looking, Camille was lucky to get him? That the money somehow made up for her defects?"

He came to a halt beside the Jeep, his expression enigmatic. "Let's just say that if Camille hadn't been traveling with approximately a metric ton of gold and jewels that history would probably have taken a different turn."

He opened the door for her, his consideration taking the sting out of his words and dampening down the knee-jerk urge to spring to her ancestor's defense. His hand cupping her elbow as she climbed into the passenger seat further distracted her. After Graham's dismissive treatment, Gabe's manners and the feeling that while she was with him she was the absolute focus of his attention were a much-needed balm.

Feeling breathless, she fastened her seat belt. As Gabe swung into the driver's seat, the cab of the Jeep seemed to shrink, suddenly claustrophobically small and disturbingly intimate.

Sarah attempted to relax as Gabe accelerated out of the garage into the murky night, but the easy camaraderie of earlier in the evening had evaporated. Bludgeoned out of existence by her usual bluntness, she thought grimly.

Minutes later, when he pulled into a parking space on the road above her rain-drenched cottage, her stomach tightened at the knowledge that whatever she and Gabe had shared would be over in a matter of seconds. "Thank you for the lift."

She fumbled at the door handle, but before she could push it wide, Gabe swung out of the cab and walked around to hold the door. Rain swirled down, shimmering in the pooling light of street lamps as she retrieved her bag.

Once she was out, Gabe closed the door with a discreet *thunk*. "I'll see you to your door." A beep and flash of lights indicated that he had locked the vehicle.

Feeling breathless and chilled after the warmth of the cab, Sarah led the way to her porch with its single glowing light. She paused in the shelter of the wide, old-fashioned porch and extracted her house key from her bag. A moment later, she pushed the door wide. The house was softly lit and comforting, with lamps burning in the sitting room. Warm air flowed out, making the night seem even colder and damper.

She glanced at Gabe, suddenly awkward. A restless part of her wished for the boldness that had arisen out of nowhere earlier in the evening. She longed to have the confidence to do what she had planned and fling herself into a wild, passionate affair, to curl her fingers into the soft lapels of his jacket, go up on her toes and kiss him. But as nice as Gabe had been in looking out for her and giving her a lift home, she was determined not to make a fool of herself by misreading the situation. "Thank you for everything. I'll collect my car in the morning."

"No problem." He produced a card from his pocket and scribbled a name and number on the back of it. "Xavier will be gone, but a receptionist will be there. She'll have your keys."

She took the card, careful not to touch his fingers, and tucked it in her bag. "You're leaving first thing?"

"I have business to attend to on Zahir."

A little desperate that he was about to leave, she searched for a reason to detain him, if only for a few seconds. The question that had consumed her earlier, resurfaced. Heart beating a rapid tattoo, she lifted her chin. "Why did you follow me when I left the lecture?"

Something flared in his gaze, the electrifying intensity she had been aware of at the reception, as if he were searching for something intangible but utterly necessary to him. As if he had found that necessary quality in *her*.

His gaze connected with hers. "I couldn't let you go."

The words sent a bolt of pure sensation through her. In that moment her mind cleared on the whole issue of risk. She had gone out tonight specifically looking for a wild fling to break herself out of the emotional rut she'd fallen into. Her mother would count it a victory if Sarah married Graham. In Sarah's mind that would be the ultimate relationship train wreck because Graham would never give her the one thing she craved: true love.

But with Gabe, on some instinctive level, she knew the opposite to be true. The connection sizzled between them. She could see it in his eyes, *feel* it with every cell of her body. There was no logic or sense to it. They barely knew each other, and yet she knew in her heart that something deep and essential was right between them.

He was edgy and utterly male, and he'd been ready to go to war for her. At times he had been grim and remote, but there had been a softness and humor she had loved. She didn't know him, and yet every instinct she possessed informed her that he was everything and more she wanted in a man.

He was perfect, and in a few minutes she was going to lose him.

She drew a swift breath. "Don't go. Not yet."

Four

Gabe said something low and soft then his mouth was on hers.

Heat and sensation seared through her, time seemed to slow and stop as she lifted up on her toes, wound her arms around his neck and fitted herself more fully against him. She logged the solid wall of muscle that was his chest, the warmth of his arms as he pulled her in close, the firm swell of his arousal.

The kiss was soft and lingering and the intimacy of it rocked her. She had been kissed before, more times than she could count, but in other kisses she had been aware of an element of recoil in the process. Either she didn't like the way her date touched her, his taste or smell, or she didn't like her date, period.

There had been times when she had wondered if she was the tiniest bit frigid, but with Gabe the details that registered were all on the plus side. He smelled clean and male and delicious and his touch and taste shivered through her senses, making her feel boneless and weak. While every other kiss she'd ever experienced had been wrong in some way, this kiss was somehow right, filling her with an absorbing, dissolving heat so that she wanted to press herself even more firmly against him.

His mouth lifted then sank again, taking her under. Dimly she was aware of the strap of her handbag slipping off one shoulder. Misty rain swirled around the enclosure of the porch, triggering disorienting flashes of the sensual dream she had experienced just that morning.

Gabe lifted his head. His gaze locked with hers. "If you want me to leave, you should say so now."

The cool separation when only moments before she had been held against the muscled heat of his body was faintly shocking. He wanted her. That thought alone was enough to anchor her, when for years she had felt rejected as a woman and intrinsically undesirable.

Now she knew that none of those past relationships had been right because she had been waiting for the deep connection she needed. It had never happened with anyone else, but through some strange alchemy it had happened with Gabe.

The knowledge filled her with dizzying relief. She had begun to think she was odd, different, that she would never marry, never have the warm family chaos, the husband and babies that were at the center of most of her friends' lives. She had begun to believe that she would never be truly loved.

It was a huge leap to go from one kiss to thinking that Gabe could be hers. Making love with him would be a risk, but *not* making love would be an even bigger risk.

She might miss her only chance to feel this way—loved and desired by the man of her choice.

Sarah touched Gabe's jaw, loving the rough feel of his five-o'clock shadow. Drawn by an impulse that had its roots in the dream, she allowed her fingers to drift over the smooth, ridged scar that marred his cheekbone.

Something flared in his eyes, gone almost as swiftly as it had appeared, then his mouth was on hers. A split second later, the world went sideways as Sarah found herself swung into his arms.

One step and they were inside her house. She heard the door slam shut then they were moving.

Gabe lifted his head. "Which way is the bedroom?"

She indicated a left turn. Moments later he carried her into the dim shadows of her room lit only by the lamp-light washing down the hall and the glow of a street-light flowing through her window. Setting her down, he shrugged out of his jacket, letting it drop to the floor. He kissed her again, drawing her against him as he slowly drew the zipper that fastened her dress down the sensitive curve of her spine. Cool air circulated against her skin as she stepped out of the dress and set to work on the buttons of Gabe's shirt, although that work was momentarily halted as Gabe dispensed with her bra and cupped her breasts.

Long dizzying seconds passed as he bent and took first one breast, then the other into his mouth, the sensation pulling every muscle tight and starting a heavy ache low in her belly. Despite the coolness of the air against her skin and the chilly sound of the rain on the windows, heat flushed her skin making her feel restless and hot.

Lifting his mouth, Gabe dispensed with the remaining buttons of his shirt and shrugged out of it, before pulling her close. Drawing in a breath at the seductive heat of skin on skin, Sarah coiled her arms around his neck and pulled his mouth to hers, the kiss deepening as he walked her backward to the bed. She felt the soft give of the mattress at the back of her knees then she sank back onto the down-filled white quilt, Gabe sprawled beside her.

He moved over her, his weight pressing her down. Little more than fifteen minutes ago she had been on the verge of saying good-night out on the porch, now they were on the verge of making love. Disorientation hit her at how fast things had moved, but the night had an odd dreamlike quality and the dizzying intensity of emotion that burst through her with every touch of his hands, his mouth, was too addictive to relinquish.

She felt his fingers tugging at her panties and shifted restlessly, helping him strip them down her legs. The faintly rough weave of his pants brushed against her sensitive skin.

Frustrated that while she was naked Gabe was still half dressed, she reached down and tugged at the fastening of his pants. She dragged the zipper down and felt the blunt, silky shape of him in her hands. He muttered something taut beneath his breath as he moved between her legs. A split second later she felt him lodged against her. Hot, irresistible sensation burst through her as she instinctively pressed against him, inviting him deeper.

He tensed and attempted to withdraw but, utterly mesmerized by a burning maelstrom of sensation, Sarah's arms coiled tighter as she pressed closer still. An agonizing second later he shoved deep and the irresistible, coiling heat shimmered and dissolved along with the night.

* * *

Long minutes later, Gabe propped himself on one elbow, his gaze in the darkened room brooding and reflective. He stroked one fingertip over her tender bottom lip in a lingering caress that sent a shiver through her. "How likely is it that you'll get pregnant?"

The question was shocking. Although it was a possibility Sarah had been turning over while she'd attempted to adjust to the intimacy of what they'd just done and the shameless way she had pressed herself against him before he'd had a chance to use a condom.

The possibility of an unplanned pregnancy. It was not a problem she had ever thought she would face. Along with the thought of a pregnancy and all that entailed, Gabe's practicality in asking the question brought her back to earth with a thump. For long minutes she had been caught up in her own very private fantasy, but with every second that passed it was becoming increasingly obvious that Gabe did not share her longings.

She swallowed against the sudden ache at the back of her throat and made an effort to dismiss the hurt. She needed to be as practical as Gabe. She had wanted to make love and they had. It had been a huge risk and, whatever the outcome, she refused to regret what had happened.

A baby. The thought that in the past few minutes they could have made a tiny human life together was stunning.

Gabe might have no interest in anything more than an interlude, *a one-night stand*, but if there was a baby, Sarah would want it. She loved kids and adored babies. She had always wanted at least one of her own, and the way things had been going she had begun to think she would never be a mother.

She drew a deep breath. Gabe's silence spoke louder than words, there was no way he wanted the complication of a baby. Since he was leaving in the morning, and he hadn't indicated that he was coming back to New Zealand, she had to assume that it was entirely possible that they would never see each other again. "Don't worry about a baby. It won't be a problem."

If she was pregnant, it was too late now; it was done. And if Gabe did not want an actual relationship with her then so be it. She would take sole responsibility for the child.

Gabe cupped her jaw, his gaze intent. What he saw in her eyes must have satisfied him. "I've never done that before, so you don't have to worry about STDs."

She suppressed the sharp hurt that Gabe was clearly used to making love with women, and the jab of guilt that he obviously thought she had taken care of contraception. "Ditto."

Something like relief flickered in his gaze. "Good."

As Gabe climbed from the bed and drew the curtains against the rain still spattering the windows, it registered that he hadn't noticed she was a virgin. That small point shouldn't have mattered, but somehow it did. Although, with the swiftness with which they'd come together, Gabe probably hadn't had time to process anything beyond the fact that they'd had unprotected sex.

As he peeled out of his boots and pants, items she hadn't given him time to fully dispense with, Sarah surreptitiously pulled back the quilt and shimmied beneath it.

Gabe, who was in the process of tearing open a foil

packet, prevented her cover up by the simple expedient of stripping back the quilt. "Don't," he said softly. "I want to remember you like this."

The finality of the words—as if they'd already said goodbye—struck her forcibly.

Despite her innate caution, while they'd been kissing, undressing, hope had formed. She and Gabe would swap numbers. He would call her from Zahir and somehow they would form a relationship. And maybe, just maybe, sometime in the misty future there would be the possibility of something real and enduring.

Tension gripped her as she watched Gabe sheath himself in the dim light. With his biceps bronzed and gleaming, chest and abs tautly muscled, he was beautiful in a fierce, completely male way and she wanted him.

But he wasn't hers. The truth was there in the faint remoteness of his gaze, a subtle distance she could feel even in the midst of passion.

As he joined her on the bed, she propped herself on one elbow and looked directly into his eyes. "Are you married?"

"No."

Relief filled her. "Good." She suspected that Gabe wasn't as free as he seemed but she didn't want to know that there was a girlfriend or significant other back on Zahir. If there was, what was between them obviously wasn't strong enough to hold Gabe. To her mind that meant it wasn't love.

Love. The concept burned through her, initiating a new tension. Everything she had felt for Gabe had been new, intense and passionate. She drew a swift breath as the reality hit home of how affected she had been by him. She didn't see how anyone could fall in love in the space of a few hours, but she had.

Her chest squeezed tight. Swallowing the impending hurt, the silly desire to cry, she leaned down and kissed Gabe, her hair sliding like a curtain around them.

The thought that she could be pregnant already made her feel even more unsettled. As his hands moved to her waist, drawing her down to him, she forced herself to forget about the possibility of a pregnancy, forget about the fact that Gabe was leaving.

If they only had one night, she was determined that it would be a night to remember.

Sarah woke to sun streaming through a gap in the curtains. Yawning, she turned over, reaching for Gabe only to find cool rumpled sheets and a pillow with an indentation. She glanced around the room. The certainty that he had gone was there in the absence of any of his clothing.

A knock at the front door had her jackknifing out of bed. Shrugging into her robe, she tightened the belt around her waist and dragged fingers through her tangled hair. Her first thought was that Gabe must have gone out for a walk, or maybe to buy some breakfast.

When she opened the door, a uniformed courier was standing on her porch with a huge bunch of dark red, perfectly formed roses.

Her mood plunging, Sarah took the flowers and set them on a side table just inside the hall while she signed an electronic pad to confirm she had received them. Closing the door, she leaned against it and stared at the beautiful, expensive bouquet. A quick check revealed there was no card.

Stomach tightening, she picked up the heavy bunch

and carried them to her small kitchen. She had received roses only twice before in her life. Roger had given her a modest bunch on her birthday, once, but they had been pink and wrapped in yellow paper with the unmistakable tag of a local supermarket. Mark had sent her one lone rose on a Valentine's Day. Neither man had thought to send her two-dozen roses that hinted at the passionate, sensual bond she now knew could exist between a man and a woman.

But then, she hadn't slept with either of them.

She found a vase large enough to hold the flowers, although a part of her didn't want to either keep them or display them just in case they did represent "goodbye."

It occurred to her then that she didn't know Gabe's full name, and she had somehow forgotten to give him her phone number. Although he knew her name and address, so it should be easy enough for him to find her.

She bent forward and inhaled the fragrance. She would stay positive, hang on to hope. All of her instincts told her that Gabe was special, that despite that touch of remoteness—a caution she well knew—he had valued their passionate hours together as much as she.

He would call; it was just a matter of time.

Gabe could not afford to contact Sarah, ever.

The thought made his mood even grimmer as he boarded his chartered flight, late.

Xavier, who had been waiting in the departure lounge, strode alongside him, his expression taut. "I thought I was going to have to come and get you."

Gabe took his seat in the small jet's luxury cabin, resignation settling in at his friend's implication. "Don't tell me, there was a GPS tracker on the Jeep."

Xavier dropped into the seat beside him. "There's always a GPS. You're the son of the sheikh, the heir apparent. If I hired vehicles that didn't have that facility, I'd be fired."

Gabe fastened his seat belt for take-off and concentrated on resisting the insane urge to disembark and drive back to the small seaside suburb where Sarah lived.

"Please tell me you won't be seeing her again."

Gabe didn't bother answering. Xavier was justifiably upset because he had been tasked with Gabe's security. He had slipped the leash and given Xavier a difficult night. But the whole point had been that Gabe had one last night to himself.

Only it had been a little more complicated than that.

He had hoped that when he made love with Sarah the attraction would lose its potency. He had been wrong. Despite the short length of time they had spent together, he still felt the force of their connection, the emotional pull, which was even more reason to leave.

As the jet leveled out, a pretty Zahiri air hostess dressed in an elegant blue uniform, her hair caught up in a glossy knot, served coffee.

Gabe set his briefcase down on the fold-down tray, flipped it open and extracted the marriage contract. Xavier pretended to be immersed in a newspaper while Gabe once again read through the list of marriage candidates. His jaw tightened as he came back to the young woman his parents had rated number one.

Dispassionately, he studied her face, which was beautiful but, to Gabe, lacking in personality. There was no hint of stormy emotions or engaging boldness. There was absolutely no evidence of the sharp, take-no-prisoners

intellect that would make life interesting. It was a face he
would be seeing on a daily basis once they were married.

Xavier put down his paper. "If you really are going
ahead with a marriage of convenience you shouldn't have
had a one-night stand with a twenty-eight year old history teacher."

"Twenty-eight?"

"Almost twenty-nine."

Controlling his irritation that Xavier had referred
to the hours Gabe had spent with Sarah as a one-night
stand, Gabe flipped to the legalese of the agreement. "I
suppose you had to do the security check."

"I was worried. You don't normally go off the grid
like that."

"Normally I'm too busy." Trying to finesse the traditional approach to finances his father clung to into a
system that would bring his country out of its financial
nosedive. Now their lack of solvency had reached a criti-
cal state, stopping a resort development vital for Zahir's
continued prosperity in its tracks.

And yet, despite his country's problems, his mind returned to Sarah. She was almost twenty-nine. The small
snippet of information was intriguing, and made sense.
She had been far too interesting to be younger and yet,
with her moonlight-pale skin and silky hair, her passionate intensity when they had made love, she had seemed
much younger. No wonder they had clicked so instantly.
Besides the college education, the fact that they were
close in age was one more thing they had in common.

As the jet gathered speed, Gabe closed out an image
of Sarah lying in a tumble of sheets, her hair spread out
over the pillow and applied himself to reading through
the fine print. He hit the clause that stipulated his bride

had to be pure, which was why each of the candidates was so young. With every year that passed, logic dictated that it was more difficult to find a suitable candidate for marriage who was still a virgin. A twenty-eight-year-old virgin was an impossibility.

Or, maybe not.

Gabe's heart slammed once, hard, against the wall of his chest as the engines reached a crescendo and the jet leaped into the air. Pressed back into his seat for the ascent, he felt electrified, every nerve ending in his body on fire as the missing piece of the puzzle that was Sarah fell into place.

She had been a virgin.

Nothing else explained her unusual behavior. She had been at once bold and shy, and she hadn't employed any exotic techniques. She had simply made love to him. In all the years he had been involved in relationships, no woman he had ever been with had ever made love to him like they meant it, including his wife.

He could kick himself. He had felt the initial constriction, noted the moment of discomfort on her face but, stunned by the knowledge that he had been so caught up in her passionate response that he had failed to protect them both, the significance of those sensations had bypassed him. Given that the first time had been over almost before it had begun, maybe he could be forgiven for the oversight.

"What's wrong?" Xavier must have picked up something in his expression. "Please tell me you protected yourself."

Eventually. Although he hadn't wanted to, and that had been a first. But from the moment he had seen Sarah at the reception he had been thrown off balance. Grimly he noted that if the jet wasn't in the air, he would have done something precipitate and obsessive, like walk off the flight and refuse a marriage arrangement that, long-term, would provide the stability and the heir both his family and Zahir needed. He would have behaved emotionally—in a way that he knew from bitter experience destroyed happiness and lives.

Letting out a breath, he forced himself to once more study Nadia's profile. He knew her family, of course. Her father was a French billionaire who had made his money in shipping. No doubt those two details had appealed to Gabe's father who, with the onset of his illness, had become a little obsessed with the legend of Sheikh Kadin. No doubt he thought there was a satisfying symmetry to the idea of Gabe marrying a shipping magnate's daughter. After all, that was how Zahir had made its money in the first place.

Gabe replied to the email, accepting the preferred candidate, Nadia Fortier.

His father had decreed a short engagement to give them time to get to know one another. A few months' grace in which to get to know and accept the woman he would marry.

And to forget Sarah Duval.

Five

Four months later Sarah double-checked the results her doctor handed her.

"You're absolutely sure I'm pregnant?"

Evelyn lifted a brow. "You're not just pregnant, you're very pregnant and I think you knew that. You should have come to see me sooner."

Caught between resignation, dismay and the dizzying sense of wonder that had gripped her over the past few weeks as she'd logged the undeniable symptoms of a pregnancy, Sarah tucked the sheet of paper in her handbag.

Of course she had noticed that she had missed her first period. But, caught stubbornly in denial, she had waited another month. When her cycle missed for the second time and she had begun to feel faintly nauseous, she had begun to accept that what she had thought would never happen had happened.

She sent Evelyn an apologetic look. "Sorry. I needed some adjustment time."

To her credit, Evelyn, who was an old friend, didn't comment on the fact that Sarah was pregnant and didn't have a husband or even a boyfriend. "I presume you want to keep the baby?"

The words were discreetly put while Evelyn pretended to be busy shuffling papers and checking something on her computer screen.

"Yes." The answer was unequivocal.

"Can you supply me with any history of the father?"

Despite bracing herself for this question, Sarah's cheeks warmed. This was the part she'd been dreading. She had done some research on the whole business of having a baby and knew that sometimes details about the father, such as blood type and genetic conditions, were important. "No."

There was a small, vibrating silence. Evelyn ducked her head, her own cheeks flushed, but not before Sarah caught the flash of compassion in her friend's eyes. Evelyn knew Sarah's past, vividly. Evelyn was supposed to be Sarah's bridesmaid at the first wedding, her maid of honor at the second. Instead, Sarah had cried on Evelyn's shoulder over men, twice.

She wouldn't be crying on Evelyn's shoulder a third time because this mistake was in a whole new league.

Sarah hadn't been sedately courted by a man she and her family and friends knew well. She'd had a wildly romantic night of passion with an exotic stranger, a one-night stand, and then he had disappeared, leaving her flat.

She had committed every mistake in the book within the space of a few hours, literally picking up a guy, having unprotected sex with him and getting pregnant, and she didn't even know Gabe's full name. All she knew was that he lived thousands of miles away on an island in the Mediterranean and that he worked for the Sheikh of Zahir. Since Gabe had been careful not to supply her with any contact details, or even his full name, it was clear that he did not want further interaction with her.

Her behavior had not just been uncharacteristic, it had been dumb, and all because she'd been seduced by a romantic dream and frightened by the thought that she would end up thirty and alone.

She should have been a lot smarter than she had turned out to be. Becoming a mother was going to have a huge effect on her life. For a start, she would have to quit her full-time teaching job, because she wanted to stay home with her child. That meant she would have to find alternative employment, something she could do from home. Although she had already come up with an idea which was, crazily enough, based on Camille's journal.

Sarah forced herself to relax. There was no need to panic. She would work it all out one step at a time. "Okay, what do I do now?"

Evelyn scribbled her signature on a form and handed it to Sarah. "You'll need to have a blood test and make an appointment to come and see me in a week's time, but you've always been in great health so I don't anticipate any problems."

She opened a drawer and took out a bunch of pamphlets, selected several and slipped them across the surface of her desk. "Do some reading, don't drink alcohol and don't take any medication unless you run it by me, not even a painkiller. If you've been feeling sick, that's normal, but if it gets too bad come and see me right away."

Evelyn pulled up a file on her laptop and tapped briskly before hitting the print button. When the copy printed out, she handed it to Sarah. "It's an application for a scan. Since it looks like you're at least four months pregnant, you should have one of those. The clinic will contact you with a date and time."

Sarah took the form. A tentative, dawning delight began to spread through her. If anything could make the baby real, this was it. "Thanks."

Slipping the paperwork inside her handbag, she pushed to her feet.

Evelyn walked Sarah to the door. "If you need to stay longer and talk, I can stall the next appointment for a few minutes. And if you just want to talk, call me at home. Anytime."

Sarah pinned a smile on her face. She had been coming to Evelyn for years. Aside from the friendship that had developed between them at university, they had the perfect doctor/patient relationship. But if Sarah had to admit to Evelyn how naive she'd been, the relationship would be permanently dented. "I'll be fine, thanks. Don't forget I have a mother."

"Of course."

The relief on Evelyn's face confirmed Sarah's thoughts. Evelyn was smart, successful and married to another doctor. They had three children, a nanny and what looked like a perfectly organized life. As compassionate as Evelyn would try to be, there was no way she could understand why Sarah had slept with Gabe.

As Sarah walked out of the medical center into the warmth of a summer's day, she felt a tiny flutter, like but-

terfly wings, in her stomach. She froze, her hand going
to her abdomen. The flutter came again and a sense of
wonder spread through her. In just a few months she
would be a mother.

Joy, heady and a little incredulous, hit her. For long
moments she simply stood on the sidewalk, foot traffic flowing around her. She didn't have everything she
wanted out of life. She didn't have a husband to love
and who would love her, but she was going to have a
baby, something she'd thought she would miss out on
altogether.

Feeling disoriented and shaky, she took dark glasses
from her bag, slid them onto the bridge of her nose and
strolled to where she'd parked the car. She unlocked the
driver's-side door, opened it and waited a few seconds
for the heat that had built up inside to dissipate before
climbing in. Instead of driving home, she drove by the
Zahiri consulate.

On impulse, she pulled into the parking lot and found
a space just outside the main entrance. Heart pounding
at the idea that had blossomed, that she should at least
think about contacting Gabe, she checked her appearance in the rearview mirror before exiting the car. Her
hair was coiled in the messy knot she had perfected and
her skin was positively glowing. Rummaging in her bag,
she found her makeup kit, retouched around her eyes and
applied fresh gloss to her mouth.

Stepping out of the car, she smoothed the loose white
shirt she had teamed with a pair of camel pants, both
items classic and stylish, but loose enough to fit comfort-
ably, given that her waist had started to thicken.

A dark-haired receptionist, different from the one she
had collected her car keys from the morning after she

had slept with Gabe, listened to her enquiry. "We don't have anyone named Gabe working here. Do you have a surname?"

Sarah explained that Gabe had only been in the country for a short time, with the sheikh's entourage.

The woman's gaze grew oddly evasive. Sarah was almost certain she knew exactly to whom Sarah was referring.

She pushed to her feet. "Just one moment."

Frowning, Sarah watched her disappear into a side office. Moments later she reappeared with a small, plump man—Tarik. Sarah's stomach dropped.

After an unsatisfactory interview in which Tarik had first pretended not to recognize Sarah, and had then feigned confusion over which Gabe she was referring to, Sarah lost her temper. "The Gabe who picked up the sword after I dropped it at the reception. The man you appeared to know very well."

There was a small silence. "Do you have a photograph of him?"

Sarah's brows jerked together at the odd question. "No."

Tarik seemed to relax at that point, his voice turning as smooth as butter. "He doesn't work for the sheikh. He was just on…assignment."

Her fingers tightened on the strap of her bag. "What does that mean?"

Tarik fixed her with a bland stare. "It means he is not in the sheikh's employ."

"So you won't help me contact him?"

"No."

Annoyed at being treated like some kind of groupie, or worse, a stalker, Sarah turned on her heel and left the consulate, aware of two sets of eyes boring into her back. She was convinced they knew exactly who Gabe was, and where he was, and that for some unfathomable reason they were protecting him.

Grimly she decided that reason was probably that Gabe was married, even though he'd said he wasn't. Maybe her judgment in sleeping with him had been more skewed than she'd thought.

Her temper, held on a tight leash for most of the interview, boiled over again as she unlocked her car door. Lately, with the pregnancy, she had noticed a tendency toward mood swings. It no doubt had something to do with the hormones rioting through her body. Whatever the cause, her personality had definitely found another gear.

Fuming, she drove home and walked into her front room. Her plan was to find the first Zahiri ornament that came to hand and smash it in the hopes that small satisfying act of destruction would make her feel better. Instead she found Graham in her house.

Graham's head jerked up guiltily. He had a sheaf of papers in his hand. "I thought you'd be at work."

Sarah dropped her bag on a side table. "Normally I would be, and—" she checked her wristwatch "—that would have given you another good two hours to steal whatever it was you came to steal."

Graham tried for a smile. "You're looking good, Sarah, positively blooming. We should go out sometime."

She couldn't believe his nerve. She noticed Camille de Vallois's journal on a coffee table, the spine broken. "You've copied the journal." And by the looks of things, he'd been cheeky enough to use her paper and copier.

"I didn't think you'd mind—"

"You mean you hoped I'd never find out."

His cheeks reddened. He glanced at his watch as if he was suddenly in a hurry. "Uh—I need to go. I'm flying out to Zahir in a few hours, so I need to pack."

Sarah pointedly held the front door open. "Good luck finding the missing dowry. And if I ever find you in my house again, I'll call the police."

Graham's expression turned decidedly unpleasant. "I won't be back. Why would I when I've got what I wanted?"

Sarah slammed the door as Graham scuttled up the drive. She hooked the chain for good measure then walked back into her tiny sitting room, picked up the journal and sat down. She took a calming breath, then another, as she heard the whine of Graham's sports car, which must have been sneakily parked outside someone else's house, accelerate away.

The interview with Tarik, followed by the altercation with Graham, had worn her out.

She strolled through to her bedroom to put away the journal, but on the way down the hallway, something went curiously wrong with her balance. Head spinning, skin flushing with perspiration, she clung to the wall for long seconds before making a dash for the bathroom.

Minutes later, she rinsed out her mouth and staggered the rest of the way to the bedroom. Up until a few minutes ago she had felt healthy and alert and even more energetic than she normally did. But now that she had finally acknowledged the pregnancy, it seemed her body had decided to catch up on a few symptoms.

Opening her closet door, she put the journal on a shelf. As she did so, she glimpsed a flash of red on the floor of the closet. The dress she had worn the night she had made love with Gabe.

Jaw clenched against another wave of nausea, she retrieved the crumpled dress and sat on the edge of the bed as she waited for her stomach to settle. She should get rid of the dress, get rid of every last association with Gabe, but a part of her couldn't. In her heart of hearts she had been sure that there was a genuine connection between them. What she'd felt and experienced had been too real to be fake.

Annoyed with herself for mooning over the past, Sarah bundled up the red dress, strode to the kitchen and jammed it into the trash.

Another wave of dizziness hit her. She gripped the kitchen counter. She felt so washed-out. Would she really be able to do this alone?

Yes. She was determined to be positive. She loved kids and she adored babies. This baby was hers and she would love it within an inch of its life. And concentrating on being a mother rather than a wife or lover suited her perfectly, because she was definitely off men!

Three days later, Sarah went for her ultrasound and stared, hypnotized, at the tiny life growing inside her.

The nurse, a cheerful middle-aged woman, peered at the screen. "Do you want to know the sex of the baby?"

Mesmerized by the clearly discernible arms and legs, the delicate, sleepy face, Sarah instantly said, "Yes."

"You're having a girl."

Sarah's throat tightened and her chest swelled. She was no longer just having a baby; she was having a daughter. She wasn't a crier. She hated crying, but these days tears seemed to well at the drop of a hat.

Smiling, the nurse handed her a wad of tissues. "I'll bet your husband will be pleased. Or did he want a boy?"

Sarah mopped her eyes and blew her nose and tried not to imagine what Gabe might want. "I don't have a husband."

She had developed a new and far more satisfying focus in life than searching for her own personal knight in shining armor. She was determined to learn all she could about childbirth and parenting, to enjoy the changes to her body, the weird cravings and the myriad discomforts. Once the baby was born, she would then put theory into practice and do her very best as a mother.

As she stepped out of the clinic into the glaring heat, the copy of the scan tucked into her bag, a tall lean guy in a suit strolled by, caught her eye and smiled. Automatically, Sarah smiled back, although she didn't know him at all. When she turned her head, he was still watching her, his expression appreciative. With a jolt, she realized he was flirting with her.

Feeling dazed, she unlocked her car. As she slid into the driver's seat she stared at her reflection in the rearview mirror. Her hair, piled as it was into a loose knot, looked tousled and sexy. Her eyes were a deep, pure blue and her skin had a definite glow, as if she was illuminated from within.

With a start she realized that despite the bouts of tiredness and sickness she had never looked better. She wasn't just attractive; she was beautiful. An odd sense of lightness assailed her. For the first time in years, her failed engagements didn't seem important. Gabe's defection was too recent to discount, but that disappointment was, also, no longer crushing.

She felt stronger, more confident. Maybe someday she

would meet a man she could fall for and who would actually fall for her in return, but if that didn't happen, she wasn't going to fret about it. The moment was freeing.

Fastening her seat belt, she started the car and pulled out into traffic. All that was left to resolve was the mystery that surrounded Gabe. She needed to decide whether or not she should allow him to be a part of her baby's life.

And find out what kind of man she had slept with.

Six

Gabe boarded his chartered flight out of Dubai, following his meeting with the construction CEO who had agreed to build the stalled resort complex on Zahir. With Gabe's engagement now formalized, a partial financial settlement had been made into Zahir's accounts and he had been able to transfer the funds, enabling the contractor to resume work.

Xavier was waiting for him in the small jet's luxury cabin. "I've been trying to call you."

Gabe frowned at Xavier's presence as he dropped into a seat beside him. "Cell phone coverage is sketchy in Buraimi, but then you knew that." His gaze sharpened. "What's wrong? Is my father okay?"

"He's fine. Your mother oversees every medical detail. He wouldn't dare not recover."

Gabe found himself grinning. "It's hard to say no to

Mom." The eldest of a family of eight and with a law degree, she had the kind of immovable, steely calm that was hard to mess with.

Xavier was silent for a moment. "Have you been in contact with the Duval woman?"

Gabe froze as he fastened his seat belt for takeoff. *The Duval woman.* As if Sarah was hardened and manipulative, when Gabe knew the opposite to be true.

A picture of the way Sarah had looked, asleep, as he'd quietly dressed and left her cottage in the early morning hours shimmered in his mind. Dark silky hair sliding over one flushed cheek, the outline of her body graceful beneath tangled bedclothes. Every muscle in his body tightened at the vivid memory of what it had felt like to make love with her, a memory he had worked hard to obliterate. "You know I haven't. What's wrong? Is she all right?"

"Uh—nothing's wrong. She's fine." There was a vibrating pause. "Tarik thinks she might be pregnant."

Gabe's heart slammed against the wall of his chest. "I thought we were past the point where there was a possibility of a pregnancy."

It was a thought that had consumed him for some weeks after they had made love. Despite the major complication a pregnancy would have been, a part of him had been crazily, irresistibly attracted to the idea that Sarah could be pregnant with his child. His fingers tightened on the arms of his seat. It had been another indication that, despite his efforts to distance himself from that night with Sarah, he had become entangled in the kind of obsessive emotion he had vowed to avoid.

Xavier shrugged. "I talked to Tarik a couple of hours ago. He practically had a heart attack over the phone."

Gabe dragged at his tie, loosening the knot. "What makes him think she could be pregnant now? It's been over four months."

"A few days ago she walked into the consulate looking for you. Why would she wait so long to do that?"

Gabe's pulse rate lifted a notch at the visual of Sarah confronting Tarik and trying to prise Gabe's contact details out of the man. Gabe would have liked to have seen that battle of wills. Out of nowhere a lightness he hadn't felt for a very long time—*four months and eleven days to be exact*—flooded him, dissolving the tension that had gripped him since spending a large chunk of the marriage settlement funds. Spending the money had sealed him even more completely into the agreement. Worse, it had made *him* feel bought and paid for. "Maybe she just wanted to contact me."

Xavier looked frustrated. "This is why you need a bodyguard. Sometimes, I think you and I live in different universes. The consulate receptionist agreed with Tarik. She thought Sarah *looked* pregnant. Something about a loose blouse and a glow."

"A glow isn't exactly evidence." Although he found himself suddenly ensnared by the idea of Sarah glowing.

"Tarik uncovered something else interesting. Sarah is a descendent of Camille de Vallois's family."

Gabe frowned. "There have got to be thousands of descendants of the de Vallois family. As I recall they were wealthy and prolific."

"Granted, but you don't normally sleep with one of them."

On edge and unsettled, Gabe glanced out of the jet's window as the glittering city and blue-green sea of Dubai receded. He knew what Xavier was getting at.

Maybe Sarah was somehow fascinated by the old legend. Maybe that had been her motivation for sleeping with him. The only difficulty with that scenario was that four months ago Sarah hadn't known he was a sheikh. She had thought he was an employee.

Added to that, she had made no attempt to contact him—until she had walked into the consulate and spoken to Tarik. For long moments, Gabe became lost in the riveting concept of Sarah, *pregnant with his child* and searching for him.

When the jet leveled out, he released his safety belt and retrieved his laptop. He opened the surveillance report that he had commissioned precisely so that Xavier would have no excuse to do so. Although he already knew Sarah's daily routine by heart, including the fact that she had recently joined a gym, changed her hairdresser and added a weekly visit to a beauty therapist. Although, the factual report, fascinating as it was, didn't interest him. It was the photographs attached that he wanted to examine. Snapshots of Sarah going about her normal life, which he had perused more times than he cared to count.

He studied Sarah wearing a sleek red suit and a pair of black-rimmed glasses that made her look corporate and outrageously sexy. Sarah in jeans and a tight sweater going shopping. Another shot where she was wearing a pink dress with a slit on one side that showed off long, tanned legs. He frowned at how increasingly alluring and feminine she looked as the months had gone by. Another more disturbing word popped into his mind—*available*.

He stared at an image of Sara sunbathing on the beach below her cottage, wearing an ultra-skimpy floral bikini. Annoyance gripped him that the PI who took the photo had spied on her when she was practically naked, even though Gabe had ordered it.

He sat back in his seat, jaw tight, annoyed at the whole concept of Sarah being available. Not for the first time it occurred to him that now that Sarah was sexually awakened she would feel free to sleep with other men.

Over his dead body.

Not that he had any rights over Sarah. But if she was pregnant with his child, that would change.

The primitive surge of possessiveness took him by surprise and formed a decision that settled smoothly into place. If Sarah was pregnant, they would work something out. She wouldn't be happy with him. He had left her, and the reason he'd had to do so was still in place. Even so, if there was a child involved, *his child*, he wasn't prepared to walk away.

The ramifications of becoming a father made his heart pound. "I'm going to New Zealand."

Xavier's head jerked up. "You can't. Your wedding date is set and besides, your father will have a stroke if he finds out you had a one-night stand with a twenty-eight-year-old history teacher."

"Twenty-nine," Gabe muttered absently, as he wrote a brief email to his personal assistant to arrange the flight. "She had a birthday a few weeks ago."

"You remembered her birthday?" There was another tense silence. "I knew it. You're falling for her."

Gabe's stomach tightened at the idea of falling in love again. "Love doesn't come into the equation. Sarah's birthday was on the security report."

"You're supposed to be trying to form a relationship with your fiancée. Nadia's smart, beautiful—most men would kill to spend just one night with her."

Gabe pressed the send button.

When the jet landed, Gabe gave in to an uncharacteristic surge of impatience and rang Sarah's number which had been conveniently supplied in the report. With the time and date difference, he didn't know if she would be at home or at work. Long seconds passed. Convinced that she wasn't home, he was about to terminate the call when she picked up, her voice husky and soft as if he'd woken her from sleep.

Gabe's stomach tightened at the thought of Sarah lying in bed. For a moment he felt tongue-tied and almost entirely bereft of English. "Sarah, it's Gabe."

There was an echoing moment of silence. "Gabe who?"

The phone slammed down, the noise loud enough to make him jerk his cell from his ear.

Xavier shot him a horrified look. "You just called her. You should let me deal with this. If she really is pregnant—"

"No. Go near Sarah Duval and you're fired."

"You can't afford a scandal."

Neither could he afford to lose a child.

Gabe called Sarah again. This time the line was engaged, which meant she had left the phone off the hook.

As he stepped outside into the hot Zahiri sun he replayed the all-too-brief conversation, the small silence then the husky curtness of Sarah's voice, as if she was hurt. Even though the evidence was sketchy, he was abruptly certain that Sarah was pregnant.

When he reached the palace, he confirmed his flight and travel arrangements and cleared his schedule for the next four days, including canceling a formal dinner with his fiancée and her parents. Feeling restless and on edge, he stepped onto the balcony of his private suite and paced.

Gripping the still sun-warmed balustrade, he stared at the smooth sweep of sea glimmering beneath the rising moon, buttery gold and huge on the horizon.

Sarah trying to contact him and hitting a wall would explain why she might not feel like talking to him now. In her mind, he had abandoned her. Worse, he had made sure she couldn't find him.

Once Sarah knew his situation, she would understand the need for discretion. She would understand why he'd had to leave her.

She was a mature, educated woman. He was certain they could work it out.

Sarah stared at the shadowy shape of the phone in the dark, shock and a sharp jolt of anger running through her. Dragging tumbled hair from her face, she flicked the switch on her bedside lamp and sat up in bed. Her digital clock said it was close to midnight. She had been asleep for two hours, more or less.

She should feel exhausted, but within the space of a couple of seconds any hint of exhaustion and nausea had been vaporized. She felt alert, her mind crystal clear, the heady charge of adrenaline still zinging through her veins.

On impulse, she took the phone off the hook in case Gabe tried to call again. Maybe that didn't make sense when just days ago she had tried to contact him. But lately she had been on a roller-coaster ride of emotions. One minute she wanted Gabe in her life, the next she recoiled from that particular weakness and didn't want to know. When she had slammed the phone down, it had been a knee-jerk reaction. Now that she'd hung up, she was beginning to wonder what, exactly, Gabe had wanted.

Could he possibly want *her*?

Her heart thumped hard in her chest. Somewhere deep in her abdomen the baby kicked. It was still the merest flutter, but it served to remind her that she had turned a corner with her thinking. She was no longer hurt and vulnerable, and she was over Gabe. There was a whole lot more at stake now than romance and passion.

Tossing the bedclothes aside, she headed for the kitchen. Now that the adrenaline was wearing off, her stomach was starting to turn somersaults again. Her mother had told her to munch on a supply of salty crackers. Since they went perfectly with the other things Sarah craved—pickles and cheese—she had complied.

After piling a plate and making herself a cup of weak tea, because now anything with milk made her stomach queasy, she strolled back to bed. While she worked her way through the crackers and tea she picked up the book of baby names she'd been reading before she'd fallen asleep. So far she had isolated fifty or so names and noted them on a pad on her bedside table.

Yawning, she picked up the pad and grimly ignored the way her mind kept constantly replaying Gabe's few words, the curtness of his voice, which had sent an automatic thrill through her. She began reading through the names she'd so far chosen, mentally linking each of the names with Duval because without a husband that would be her baby's surname.

Hours later, the doorbell chimed, pulling Sarah out of a restless sleep. Belting on her robe, she dragged fingers through her hair and hurried to the door. Her heart sped up at the breathless thought that it could be Gabe, that the reason he had rung was that he was back in New Zealand and wanted to see her again.

Flinging open the door she was met by an enormous basket of fragrant red roses that matched the other bunches filling her porch. A short, bald deliveryman stared at her with undisguised curiosity as he requested her signature for the flowers.

Feeling dazed, confused and angry—because the dark red, deeply fragrant tea roses sent from the same expensive florist that had delivered the last lot, had to be from Gabe—Sarah scribbled her name. When the deliveryman had driven away, she lugged the flowers inside. After a brief search, she found a note attached to the enormous basket filled with roses and boxes of expensive chocolates. When she opened the note she stared blankly at Gabe's full name, which was unexpectedly long, and a number.

A red mist obscured her vision for long seconds. She was finally over him and *now* he decided to provide his phone number? When the mist cleared she found herself out on her deck, the myriad shreds of paper that had once been the note whipping away in the wind.

Legs suddenly weak, she walked back inside and sat down. Her skin kept going hot then cold. Her heart was beating way too fast. Rage, she decided, was definitely not good for the baby. Taking a deep breath, Sarah stared at the small fortune in roses and chocolates. She felt stunned that after all this time Gabe had decided not only to contact her, but apparently, to woo her.

Squashing the weak, wimpy kernel of hope that was unfurling irresistibly inside her, she decided that if Gabe had wanted to send her roses, he was too late.

Just like he was way late sending his contact details.

If he had genuinely cared for her and valued her, he would have given her his number months ago, or showed up at her door. Neither of those things had happened. He hadn't even bothered to check to see if she had gotten pregnant.

She went still inside. Or maybe he finally had.

That would explain the flowers and the sudden desire to be in contact, which, now that she was thinking straight, smacked of damage control.

Mood plummeting, she unconsciously cradled her abdomen, protecting the small life inside. She frowned at the thought that Tarik had seen through her visit to the consulate, that he had been suspicious enough to contact Gabe. The scenario seemed a likely explanation for both the call and the roses, given Gabe's unreliable behavior in disappearing so completely after their one night together.

Pushing to her feet, she decided that under those circumstances she didn't want the roses Gabe had deliberately chosen to remind her of the night they had spent together.

She began ferrying the roses back out onto the porch. She would give them to the pretty little church down the road, and the chocolates could go to the rest home near her school. If Gabe thought he could charm her and buy her off so she wouldn't make trouble, he could think again.

The following morning, just as she'd finished dressing for work, a knock at the door made Sarah tense. Assailed by a curious sense of déjà vu, as if she would find the same deliveryman with a new consignment of flowers, she opened the door. When she saw Gabe, she froze, too shocked to speak.

Before she could slam the door, he jammed his foot in place and planted one large palm flat on the door, holding it open. "I just need a few minutes of your time."

Chest tight, heart pounding, she did her best not to be mesmerized by his amber gaze or his fascinating scar. She was fiercely glad she had made an effort with her hair, which was wound up in a sexy knot that showed off the new caramel streaks her hairdresser had insisted she try. She was also wearing a high-waisted pale turquoise dress that was not only short enough to show off her legs, but also cleverly disguised the thickening at her waist. "You sound like a salesman."

"Technically, I'm an accountant, not a salesman."

The freely given fact about his life startled her enough that she almost weakened and let him in before she remembered that was one of the ways he had gotten her before. He had told her he had gone to Harvard to study business and she had been silly enough to think that with the prosaic nature of both of their occupations they had something in common. Determined to ignore the fascination of a man who looked like a battle-hardened warrior but had an affinity for figures—*and who had been a breathtaking lover*—she kept a firm grip on the door. "Why are you here?"

His gaze locked with hers for a burning moment that transported her back to a pitch-black night, rain pounding on her window, a breathless tangle of sheets and the heat of his skin against hers...

"I had to see you."

For a split second she was startled enough by the flat, declarative timbre of his voice that she almost weakened.

It almost seemed as if he had missed her and really had desperately needed to see her.

He frowned at her stubborn lack of response. "Did you get my roses?"

"I did."

"Let me guess, you gave them away."

"They were not exactly a happy reminder, since you left without saying goodbye and haven't bothered to keep in touch."

"But you knew I had to leave."

And she'd known that there were no promises made, on either side. Avoiding his gaze and concentrating instead on a point somewhere to the right of one mouthwatering cheekbone, she tried to nurture the fiery anger that flared whenever she considered just how much time had passed. But it was a fact that the night had been what it was: two people recognizing a mutual attraction and agreeing to sleep together. The only problem was she had been emotionally involved from the beginning.

"Thanks for reminding me." She glanced at her watch, which had a pretty turquoise band to match her dress. She tried to look as if she really was in a hurry even though the school term had ended days ago, and all she needed to do for the day was prep work for next term. "Now if that's all you have to say, I think you should go. I need to leave for work in just a few minutes." Besides that, she was beginning to feel nauseous and dizzy all over again.

Gabe's gaze seemed to pierce her, pinning her in place. "You're still working?"

His voice sounded oddly muffled, as if it were coming from a distance, although the thing that concerned her most was that something weird was happening to her vision. Vaguely, she realized she had lost her grip on the door and that Gabe had taken advantage of that fact by swinging it wide-open. Stumbling slightly, she reached for the solidity of the wall. "Why wouldn't I be?"

"I checked with your school. The receptionist said the school holidays had started."

Outrage that he had been sneaking around, poking into her life was tempered by a scary delight that he had wanted to do so. Suddenly, Gabe was close enough that she could feel the warmth of his body. It seemed the most natural thing in the world to clutch at one shoulder in a bid to stay upright. "This doesn't mean I've forgiven you." She tried to be crisp and stern, but the words sounded muffled.

His arm came around her waist. Just as everything faded to black she heard him mutter, "Damn, you are pregnant with my child."

When she came around she was lying on her couch in the sitting room and Gabe was in her house.

Tense and on edge that he had slipped past all of her defenses she cautiously levered into a sitting position. Apparently the sluggish maneuver had been way too fast, because her head started to spin again.

Gabe handed her a glass of water, which she would have refused on principle if she wasn't so thirsty all the time, and right now her mouth was as dry as a desert. Draining the glass, she set it down on the coffee table and glared at him. She was suddenly glad she had gotten rid of the roses, and hadn't allowed herself to weaken and keep any. "I don't remember inviting you into my house."

"That would be because you were too busy fainting." He loomed over her, the dark jeans and loose shirt he wore making him look lean and muscular and vital, while she felt limp and rung out. "I found your doctor's number by the phone and made an appointment." He consulted his watch. "If we leave now we might just make it."

"I don't need a doctor, there's nothing wrong with me—"

"You're pregnant."

She crossed her arms over her chest, which successfully minimized her tiny bump. "What makes you think I'm pregnant?"

Gabe dragged distracted fingers through his hair, making him look disheveled, younger and infinitely cuter. "Tarik."

Sarah's jaw tightened. That little man. It was a further confirmation she should never have gone near the consulate.

Gabe's gaze flashed broodingly over her. "Are you pregnant?"

Heat filled her cheeks. She couldn't lie. No matter how much she wanted to conceal the truth and keep the baby her secret. "Yes."

Seven

Forty minutes later Sarah was sitting in Evelyn's office while Gabe stood at a window, staring out at a slice of suburban Kilbirnie.

Evelyn strolled back into the room, throwing Gabe a glance filled with thinly veiled curiosity. Despite the fact that Sarah was still unhappy with Gabe and the way he had bulldozed her into seeing Evelyn, she couldn't help but feel a tiny glow of satisfaction that he was with her. If nothing else, it proved to Evelyn that while Sarah might have had bad luck with men in the past, at least this time she had chosen one who was certifiably gorgeous.

Evelyn handed Sarah a slip of paper with the results of her urine test. "It's not the best news. Your blood sugar is high, which makes you pre-diabetic. That accounts for the dizzy spells. It happens to some women in pregnancy."

Sarah stared at the test result. "That would also explain the thirst."

Evelyn gave Sarah a sharp look. "From now on you need to call me about anything unusual that happens. You'll need to manage your diet and I want you to have regular blood tests." Rummaging in her desk she found a diet sheet, which Gabe commandeered.

Gabe sent her a narrow-eyed glance then began asking Evelyn rapid-fire questions that indicated he had studied up on pregnancy. Evelyn crossed one elegant leg over the other and sat back in her chair, visibly preening as she smoothly answered his every question. Beginning to feel sidelined, even though she was the patient, Sarah pointedly got to her feet.

Evelyn stopped midsentence and blushed. Gabe instantly rose and cupped Sarah's elbow, in case she needed steadying. She didn't, she felt fine now, but it wasn't such a bad thing for Evelyn to understand that Gabe was here for her. Although the fact that Sarah should want to make any kind of statement at all was ridiculous because it smacked of jealousy.

When they reached Gabe's Jeep, he helped her up into the passenger seat. "You don't need to be jealous."

Sarah busied herself fastening her seat belt to disguise the fact that she was blushing furiously. "Why on earth would I be jealous?"

There was an odd, tense silence then Gabe closed her door with a soft *thunk*, walked around the bonnet and slid behind the wheel.

Enclosed in the intimacy of the Jeep the one burning question she hadn't had time to ask pushed to the fore. Jaw taut, she stared at Gabe's faintly hawkish profile as he turned into traffic. "Why are you here?"

He had already said he'd suspected she was pregnant, but she would have thought that news would make him run, not come back to her.

"If you're pregnant with my child that changes things."

"What things, exactly?"

He braked for a set of traffic lights. "I'm engaged to be married."

Fury channeled through her. If she could have found something to break in that moment, she would have broken it. Her reaction upset her. This unstable, passionate creature she seemed to be turning into wasn't her. She was normally calm and collected; she thought things through. She did not fly into rages. "I knew it. Although my guess was that you were married."

His brows jerked together. "I do not have affairs."

"But you cheated on your fiancée."

"I wasn't engaged at the time."

Her heart pounded even harder. What Gabe had said should have made the situation better, so why did it feel worse? "Let me get this right. You had sex with me then you went back to Zahir and got engaged. At least that explains why you never bothered to call."

He'd had more exciting options than a twenty-eight-year-old history teacher.

Her jaw set. "If you got engaged so quickly, you must have known your fiancée already."

Gabe pulled into her driveway. "No. It was an arranged marriage."

Horror transfixed her. "So that's why you slept with me. It was a last fling." She dragged at her seat belt, trying to unfasten it, but the mechanism wouldn't cooperate.

Gabe half turned in his seat, frowning, which only made him look more gorgeous. "It wasn't like that."

She fought against the lure of his fierce, warrior's gaze. "How was it then?"

There was a vibrating silence. "You know exactly how it was between us."

He tried to help her with the seat belt. Incensed, she pushed his hands away. "I can do this. I'm used to doing things on my own."

"You're not on your own any longer."

Even though she didn't want to feel anything at all for Gabe, his flat statement sent a dangerous hope spiraling through her. He had used the word *was* with his marriage, as if it was in the past tense. Added to that fact, he *could* have stayed on Zahir and simply ignored her. Instead he was here, *because* she was pregnant, taking charge, getting involved.

She stared at him, feeling crazily emotional, still angry but also on the verge of tears. "So how was it, exactly, between us?"

"Like this." Gabe cupped her jaw and out of nowhere the humming, tingling attraction she'd fought to suppress burst into fiery life.

He lowered his mouth, and foolishly she tossed away any thoughts of being sensible and controlled and let him kiss her.

Gabe closed Sarah's front door behind him and followed her into her sitting room. The heat that had surged through him at the kiss was still pulling every muscle in his body taut. But, aware of how badly he had mishandled things so far, he grimly controlled the need that had hit him.

As she opened French doors to let a cooling breeze in, he noticed a pad on the coffee table. Picking it up, he examined a list of names. "Tiffany, Tanesha, Tempeste…" He glanced at Sarah as she strolled out of the kitchen with two glasses of water in her hands. "Are these names for the baby?"

Setting the water down, she snatched the pad from his fingers. "They're just ideas."

"Any favorites so far?"

She snapped the pad closed. "It's just at the formulation stage. Names are important. You can't just choose any old thing."

While Sarah jammed the pad into the drawer of an antique sideboard, Gabe strolled to the French doors that opened onto a tiny deck and stared at the view over Wellington's harbor and hills. The fact that he was going to be a father hit him again, even more strongly than when Sarah had fainted. The situation was unbelievably complicated because it involved his commitment to Nadia and his country. But Sarah carrying his child changed everything.

He desperately needed to order his thoughts, to think like a Sheikh of Zahir and control the dangerous, possessive emotions that surged through him.

He needed to provide for Sarah and the baby, therefore the only possible solution was marriage. In order to marry Sarah, he would have to end his current engagement and solve Zahir's financial problems another way.

Given that his father would finally be a grandfather, and with the possibility of a future male heir to the sheikhdom in the pipeline, Gabe did not foresee that his father would hold to his stance against foreign investment.

His mind made up, Gabe turned from the view. Sarah was busy plumping cushions and tidying magazines. As she straightened, sexy tendrils of dark hair clung to her flushed cheeks, making her look both gorgeous and vulnerable. The light fabric of her dress swung against her abdomen, giving him his first real glimpse of the gentle swell of her belly. Another surge of fierce possessiveness hit him, and he frowned. Zahir's financial situation, tricky as it was, would not be a problem, but if he wasn't vigilant, what he was feeling could be. Marriage was a solution, but it could not be an unstable, emotionally based, marriage. Like the arrangement with Nadia Fortier, this too would be a marriage of convenience.

"So," he said carefully, "you're having a girl."

Sarah took a deep breath, repressing an uncharacteristic flash of temper that Gabe was extracting information from her about the baby before she was quite ready to tell him. "That's what showed up on the scan."

A curious emotion darkened his expression. Was it disappointment? Instantly she was up in arms on behalf of her child, a female baby who no doubt, in his country, was not as celebrated as a male child.

"Evelyn said you have a copy of the ultrasound. I'd like to see it."

He watched the video file through without a word then almost immediately replayed it again.

He closed her laptop. "The baby changes things. We need to make arrangements."

Her heart pounded out of control at his words, because in that moment she realized he was going to suggest the one thing she had wanted from him over four months ago: a relationship.

Although she wasn't sure how she felt about any of that now. Half of her was melting inside, teetering on the brink of hope, the other half still blazing mad that he had left her alone for so long. "What did you have in mind?"

He extracted a platinum card from his pocket.

The temper she had been trying to keep a lid on spilled out. "If you think you're going to start paying my bills, you can think again."

Before he could stop her, she grabbed the card, marched out on the deck and threw it over the side, down onto the lawn below. "I don't want your money, so you can forget it. Forget me—"

"I can't." With a swift movement, he pulled her toward him so that she found herself plastered against his chest.

His mouth came down on hers. She could have ducked her head or pulled away, but her precarious mood had taken another swing, from fury straight to desire. She didn't like what was happening. She didn't want his money. But after the sweet, tender moments in his Jeep, which had spun back the clock, with every cell in her body she wanted him to kiss her again.

Long, dizzying minutes later, she pulled free. Her mouth tingled; her body was on fire. She loved that he still wanted her, but they had been in this place once before. That time she had gotten pregnant. Before anything else life-changing happened, she had to be clear about whether or not they had a chance at the one thing that was important to her in a relationship: love. "Where, exactly, are you in this scenario?"

She finally identified the glimpse of emotion in his eyes that had baffled her from the moment she'd first seen him at her door—not quite cool detachment, but wariness. "I'm proposing marriage."

Her legs went weak at his blunt statement. "What about your fiancée?"

"First I'll need to go back to Zahir and terminate the agreement with Nadia."

The word *terminate* sent a chill through her. Had he not felt anything for his fiancée? At the name Nadia, alarm bells rang. Sarah walked back inside and sat down, her legs feeling wobbly. She had read something about an engagement in Zahir online. Suddenly the way Tarik and the consulate receptionist had behaved in protecting Gabe began to make perfect sense.

Gabe had said he was an accountant. It was possible he simply worked for the sheikh as part of his business team, but she was beginning to think Gabe was something more than that.

She remembered the piece of paper with Gabe's full name on it, which she had ripped up and tossed away before she'd read it properly. She thought she might have glimpsed the name Kadin somewhere. Her stomach plunged as a wild notion occurred to her, a notion that made sense of all the cloak-and-dagger behavior surrounding Gabe's identity and whereabouts. "Who are you, exactly?"

"My full name is Sheikh Kadin Gabriel ben Kadir. I'm not the ruling sheikh. That's my father, but I will rule one day."

Eight

Gabe, *Sheikh Kadin Gabriel ben Kadir,* insisted he take her to lunch while they talked over the situation. Too shocked by his announcement to refuse, Sarah found herself courteously helped into a gleaming Jeep. As Gabe pulled away from the curb, she took better note of the vehicle, which was brand-new and luxurious. Now, too late, all the subtle clues about him registered, like the way he had spoken to Tarik—not as a subordinate, but as someone in command. The fact that he'd had accommodations at the consulate, and that he'd gone to Harvard. Of course he was a member of Zahir's ruling family.

His gaze touched on hers. "How do you feel?"

"I'll feel fine when you explain why you didn't let me know who you are."

She noticed they were heading away from the city into the wilder hill country.

Gabe stopped for an intersection. "The same way you didn't let me know you're an ancestor of Camille's?"

She flushed at the quiet statement, although it wasn't as if she had concealed *her* identity. "How did you find that out? No, wait, let me take a wild guess. The son of a sheikh, with bodyguards and an impenetrable security force field around you? I'm betting you had me investigated."

"We had unprotected sex—"

"So you had to find out exactly who you had gotten entangled with." A horrified thought occurred to her. "I suppose you thought I was some kind of adventurer, maybe even a journalist."

He turned into a very beautiful, secluded drive that, from the signage, led to an exclusive private resort. "I didn't tell you I was a sheikh because I thought all we would share was the one night. And I knew you were exactly what you said, a history teacher, but the investigative process went ahead because security protocols still needed to be satisfied."

"And you were worried about a pregnancy." Her fingers tightened on the strap of her handbag as he parked beneath a shaded portico and a uniformed valet opened her door. "If you had left me your contact details, you could have saved yourself the trouble. I would have told you."

There was an uncomfortable silence as she climbed out of the Jeep. Gabe handed the keys to the valet. They were shown to a restaurant with a fabulous cliff-top view of the ocean. As he took a seat opposite her, she glanced around at the other diners. They were without exception beautiful, very well-groomed people with perfect tans. Most of them, even the men, were dressed in shades of

white and cool pastels. Dressed as she was in vibrant turquoise, with her hair wisping damply around her face,
all of the elegant restraint made her feel overly bright.
It shouldn't have mattered, but the restaurant suddenly
made her see the gulf in lifestyles that existed between
her and Gabe.

"What's wrong?"

She frowned, hating that she was actually allowing
herself to be stressed-out by surroundings that were formal and just a little pretentious. "I can't relax in this
place. What if I need to be sick?" Just the thought made
her feel queasy.

His gaze sharpened. "Do you feel unwell?"

"A little. It comes on suddenly."

The waiter who was delivering beautiful leather-
bound, gold-embossed menus, blanched. Within minutes Gabe had canceled their reservation and the valet
had delivered the Jeep to the portico. Gabe opened the
passenger-side door, but instead of simply helping her
up, he clasped her waist and boosted her into her seat.

Breathlessly, she released her hold on his shoulders.
"I could have gotten in by myself."

"Since we're engaged, I thought we should start getting used to the idea of being a couple."

She blinked at the subtle way he was trying to bull-
doze her into agreeing to marry him. "I haven't said
yes yet."

He released her, but there was a curious relief in his
gaze as if he liked that she wasn't jumping at his proposal. Although, she wasn't so sure *she* liked the idea
that if they were to marry he would be happy with a certain distance in their relationship.

When Gabe slid behind the wheel, she directed him to

a small beachside café in Lyall Bay that was casual and cheerful, with enough background noise that they could have a conversation without being overheard.

Gabe shrugged out of his jacket and dragged off his tie. With the sea breeze ruffling his hair, he looked breathtakingly handsome. While they ate he asked questions about her family and supplied details about his. It shouldn't have surprised her that he knew her cousin, Laine—who had sent Sarah the journal—and who was married to the Sheikh of Jahir, a distant relative of Gabe's. But the fact that he was close to that branch of her family was reassuring. As big a leap as it was, it somehow made it easier to imagine being married to the next Sheikh of Zahir.

Marriage to Gabe. For a split second, her heart pounded out of control. Her last two attempts at getting married had both ended in disaster and she couldn't quite believe that this one would work out.

When they'd finished, Gabe suggested they take a walk on the beach. When he clasped her hand in a loose hold, a dangerous thrill went through her because even if Gabe didn't feel the romance of what they were doing, she did, and she was afraid of being too happy. Her experience of happiness was that once you thought you had it in your grasp, it was snatched away. "Are you certain you want marriage?" Taking a breath, she offered him an alternative that would dispense with the need for a relationship altogether. "Sharing custody is an option."

Gabe stopped and pulled her into a loose hold, his gaze oddly fierce. He hooked a loose strand of hair behind one ear, the small possessive gesture sending another sharp little thrill through her. "We're both mature,

educated people. There's no reason we can't have a…
successful marriage."

Sarah frowned at the way Gabe framed marriage, as if
it was something one had to be qualified for, even while
his measured response reassured. After all, with a baby
on the way, if she was going to marry, she needed her
husband to be responsible and trustworthy.

When Gabe dipped his head, she allowed the kiss and
tried not to love it too much. Reluctantly, she planted her
palms on his chest and kept her gaze fixed on the pulse
jumping along the side of his jaw, because if she looked
at his mouth or into his eyes, she would kiss him again.
"We can't make love until…things are settled."

"Until you've agreed to marry me."

Her chin came up and this time she met his gaze.
"Yes."

It was a fact that they couldn't get engaged until Gabe
had ended his current arrangement. And Sarah knew
better than anyone, a lot could go wrong between an
engagement and the altar.

Two weeks later, Sarah, finding her state of relationship limbo a little too lonely after Gabe had gone back
to Zahir went online to indulge her new favorite hobby,
searching out news about Zahir and the ruling family.

During the two days they had spent together, they
had eaten out and gone for walks. Gabe had sketched in
brief details of his life, including the startling fact that
he was a widower. When he'd flown out they'd agreed to
stay in contact by phone. However, he hadn't called for
a whole week now, and the silence after the long, cozy
calls had her worried even though he had mentioned the
possibility of sketchy cell phone coverage. With time

passing she was beginning to have flashbacks to the silent, empty months that had followed the one night they had spent together.

Worse, she was beginning to think she had been foolishly optimistic in trusting that Gabe would choose her over Nadia Fortier. She needed to know more about his engagement, even if it was just internet gossip. And she needed to know more about the wife he had lost.

Her mother, who made a habit of dropping in unexpectedly, walked through the door, just as Sarah found a reference site. Hannah, who was naturally suspicious of Gabe, paused beside the screen, which was currently displaying a dated story about Gabe's engagement. "If you were having a boy, he would have put a ring on your finger immediately."

Sarah blinked at the flamboyant outfit her mother was wearing. A saffron-yellow dress over blue leggings. Cobalt-blue earrings made her short, spiked blond hair look even more startling. "What makes you say that?"

Hannah fished in her bag and placed cold cups of fresh fruit smoothies on the table. "Stands to reason. The sheikhdom is patriarchal, so only male children can rule, specifically the first male child. If the baby was a boy, he would be the next sheikh."

Sarah picked up her smoothie, took a sip and decided she would have to tell her mother the truth. "Gabe proposed. I'm the one who hasn't agreed, yet."

Hannah stared at her as if she'd just landed from Mars. "I thought you wanted to marry him?"

"I do." But only if Gabe truly valued her and their baby girl. Only if there was the possibility of love.

Hannah dug two salad rolls out from the depths of her bag and plunked them down on the table. "You've wanted to get married for years. Now you're dangling one of the most eligible, *hot* men on the planet?" she sat down and peeled plastic wrap off a roll. "Sometimes I don't know you."

With difficulty Sarah refrained from pointing out that her mother had just expressed two conflicting views about Gabriel. "Is it such a bad thing to not want to make another mistake?"

Too irritable to eat, she searched a site she normally never bothered with, because it was full of the kind of magazine articles and sensationalized gossip that normally didn't interest her. Moments later she found a short article posted just two days ago. She stared at a photo of Nadia Fortier in a skimpy bikini lying on a dazzling beach, a glass of champagne in one hand.

Nadia was accompanied by a broad-shouldered, dark-haired man who had his back to the camera. Sarah's heart stuttered to a halt in her chest. It looked like Gabe, and the text confirmed it. Apparently, Gabe and Nadia were spending some quality alone-time at a secret hideaway in Tuscany before the wedding.

Sarah pushed to her feet so fast the chair went flying. So much for angsting about Gabe's dead wife, when it was the gorgeous young fiancée she should have been worrying about.

At the periphery of her vision she was aware of her mother, staring at her with a frown. Sarah righted the chair, too focused on Gabe's blatant betrayal to try to appear normal or calm.

She had begun to trust him again. She had liked his phone calls, especially when he'd called late at night and she'd been snuggled up in bed.

His behavior during their two days together had made

her think he would be a wonderful father. She had seen it in his absorption with all the aspects of her pregnancy. She had loved it when he had fussed over her when she'd felt tired and ordered takeout. The next day he had insisted on stocking her pantry with healthy low-fat food.

But it had all been a smokescreen. He had lied. He hadn't gone back to Zahir to make any kind of arrangement that would benefit her and the baby. He was spending his time wining and dining his beautiful, slim fiancée at some swanky Italian *castello*.

And in that moment Sarah knew why she had been both ecstatic and miserable for the past two weeks. It wasn't just that her hormones had been running riot. She had been busy falling head over heels in love with Gabe all over again—the father of her child and a man who would be marrying someone else in three months' time.

Her mind was spinning. She could scarcely believe how completely Gabe had deceived her. Although this kind of betrayal had happened to her before.

Sarah glared at the grainy, blurred photo, which had obviously been taken with a telephoto lens, and clicked on the mouse to close the site. Caught between fierce anger and utter misery, she walked out onto her small deck, barely registering the humid grayness of the day, which was a whole lot different from the arching blue sky and blistering heat of Tuscany. A brisk wind laced with spits of rain flattened her dress against her body and sent her hair flying. So much for her improbable daydreams of moving to Zahir, of Gabe really and truly falling for her once they had time to spend together.

Trying to stay calm, she walked back into her sitting room, which was cluttered with baby paraphernalia: a pretty white bassinet and piles of bright fluffy toys. She picked up a pink bear Gabe had sent, and which was so ridiculously large it occupied its own chair. Fury boiling over, she marched the bear through to the spare room and jammed it in the closet, out of sight.

Slamming the door, she leaned against it, breathing hard.

Hannah, who had been making tea in the kitchen poked her head around the corner, looking concerned. "Are you all right?"

"Yes." No. "Eat your lunch, I'll be out soon. Promise."

Maybe the photo and the article hadn't portrayed the absolute truth. She had to stop reacting emotionally and start operating on the facts. The only way she could reliably gather facts was to go to Zahir.

Returning to the computer, she found a travel site and searched for fares. Once she had made bookings, she felt shaky but glad she had acted. She had lost two potential husbands because she had not cared enough to actively claim her man. But this time was different. Her heart and her baby's future happiness were both at stake.

She was over sitting quietly at home. Whether Gabe liked it or not, she was joining him on Zahir.

In just two days' time she would no longer be Sheik Kadin Gabriel ben Kadir's guilty secret.

Nine

Gabe walked into Gerald Fortier's office in Paris flanked by Xavier and Hasim, Gabe's personal assistant, just ten minutes short of midnight. They were all wearing the formal business attire of Zahir: well-cut suits, white shirts with ties and white kaffiyeh headdresses fastened with black rope *agals*. Kadin's *agal* was differentiated by the badge of his family, a lion rampant.

This was a meeting he had demanded ten days ago, after he'd received information that Nadia was not staying with an aunt in the South of France as her family had claimed but instead was shacked up with an Italian count in Tuscany. Fortier, clearly aware that Gabe could declare the marriage contract null and void on the basis of it, had ducked the meeting until now.

Gabe presented his ID to a doorman who seemed mesmerized by his scar, the headdress and the entourage.

Seconds later, they stepped into the elevator to the penthouse suite. When they emerged, Fortier was standing at a large plate-glass window, staring out at the spectacular view of Paris at night and the glittering landmark of the Eiffel Tower.

Fortier turned to face Gabe. As always the older man's expression was smooth and urbane, although when he noted the kaffiyehs, something usually reserved for formal or ceremonial occasions, his dark gaze became wary. He consulted his wristwatch, as if he were in a hurry to leave despite the late hour. "You're lucky you caught me, I have a plane to catch."

"To Tuscany?"

Fortier's expression paled as he indicated they should sit down on the comfortable black leather chairs grouped around a coffee table.

Gabe ignored the offer of a seat. He produced a photocopy of a snippet from a French newspaper where Fortier had stated Gabe was holidaying in Tuscany with his daughter. "You know very well I've been in New York and the United Arab Emirates for the past few days."

Fortier placed the page on the coffee table. "It was a solution. Damage control."

"Only if I still wished to marry your daughter."

Fortier stiffened. "There's no reason our agreement can't stand, especially since a substantial partial payment has been made. The agreement is sealed."

"Not any longer."

Fortier plowed on as if Gabe hadn't spoken. "Of course I can compensate you for a certain…breach of the conditions."

The breach being that Nadia was no longer a virgin and, according to the report Gabe had received, hadn't been for quite some time. Gabe also happened to know that Gerald Fortier had been well aware of that fact when he'd signed the marriage agreement.

Until Gabe had spent that one night with Sarah he hadn't realized just how much integrity in his relationships mattered. "I'm afraid," he said softly, "that part of the agreement is nonnegotiable."

There was a small, tense silence. Fortier's gaze flickered over Xavier and Hasim, who were flanking Gabe in an unmistakably military fashion. Fortier jerked at his tie. "In that case I will require immediate and full repayment of the funds you've received."

Gabe kept his expression neutral. With the small constitutional change Gabe's father had made, repaying Fortier would not be a problem. "You'll have the money as soon as the finance I've arranged with a New York bank is approved. In return I'll make certain that the information that Nadia is having an affair is not leaked to the press."

Fortier's face went dead white then flushed bright red. "Thank you."

The man's momentary loss of control informed Gabe that, for all his faults, Fortier cared about his daughter's reputation.

Turning on his heel, Gabe led the way to the elevator. Within an hour he was back on the small jet he had chartered. The engagement was now null and void, although he couldn't allow himself to celebrate just yet.

His mother was quietly over the moon that Gabe wanted to marry a New Zealand girl and that there was a grandchild already on the way. Breaking the news to the general populace of Zahir, however, would be a more delicate issue.

Preparations for the wedding were almost complete. Invitations had been sent and hotels had been booked out. The cancellation was a matter that would have to be handled by the public relations experts. Although Gabe was certain that once the tourism minister got hold of the fact that Sarah was a descendent of Camille de Vallois, he would leverage the information into a wave of public approval that would smooth over the fact that he was changing brides.

Grinning at the thought that finally there was a practical application for the romantic story of Kadin and Camille, he dropped into a leather seat. Taking out his cell he logged the string of missed calls from Sarah and tried to call her before the jet taxied onto the runway. It was something he hadn't been able to do while in the remote hill country of Buraimi.

When the call went to voice mail and Sarah didn't respond on her cell, he checked his messages. There were two from Sarah. He listened to the cool, low register of her voice as she requested that he contact her. The last message had been left four days ago.

Grimly, he tried calling Sarah again. When there was no reply, he turned his cell off. If there was an issue with the pregnancy, Sarah would have said so in one of the two messages she'd left, and which he hadn't been able to pick up because there was no cell phone service in Buraimi.

Xavier, who had been talking to the pilot, dropped into the seat beside him. "A problem?"

"Nothing I can't handle."

He'd been away from Sarah for two weeks. Two weeks too long. He had missed her.

His jaw tightened at just how much, because a part

of him didn't want to be subject to the whims of desire and the havoc it could wreak.

While the other part of him couldn't wait to have her back in his arms.

Zahir glittered beneath the scorching noonday sun as Sarah paid the bellhop who had delivered her bags then strolled through the cool, spacious hotel suite she had reserved for the next ten days.

After changing into a white cotton dress, she collected her camera and a notebook and took the elevator to the ground floor. Evelyn had reluctantly given her the all-clear to travel after her blood test had been much improved. Now that Sarah had moderated her diet the dizzy spells had abated and she was feeling much more energetic.

She strolled out onto one of Zahir's narrow, quirky streets, loving the heat and the quaint lime-washed buildings clinging to the hills and cliffs that rimmed most of the bay. Zahir was also home to a cluster of beautiful resorts, all owned by the sheikh. The resorts had all been built to blend with the historic old city and looked more like ancient villas and palaces than actual hotels.

Lifting her camera, she took several shots to catch the panoramic view then started down the steep hill to the main street, which ran along the shoreline and was famous for its cafes and souks. As she strolled, she frowned at the sight of a sign in Zahiri and English congratulating Sheikh Kadin on his upcoming marriage. Festive ribbons and lights strung across the streets and huge planters spilled richly scented flowers in celebration. Her mood dropping, she lifted her camera and snapped a photo. If she had wanted confirmation that the wedding had not been called off, this was it.

The zeal she'd had to gather information then fling it at Gabe when next he contacted her abruptly flatlined. It was all very well playing detective, but it didn't feel so good when the results seemed to confirm her worst fears. Feeling deflated, she stopped to buy a cold drink at a small bustling café.

The pretty English waitress who served her was breezy and chatty and happy enough to answer the few halting questions Sarah asked.

She set a cool drink in front of Sarah. "Almost no one's actually seen Nadia. I think her family are keeping her under wraps until the day, you know? Although, if you go online you'll find a few photos. She's young and drop-dead gorgeous. Apparently she used to be on social media until the engagement was set in concrete, then—" she made a slicing gesture across her throat "—nothing."

Sarah took a desultory sip of her drink, which was a delicious sweet-sour concoction of plum and lemon, laden with ice. "I guess Gabe—the sheikh, can be controlling."

The waitress gave her a disbelieving look. "I was talking about Nadia's father. Kadin is a whole different kettle of fish, a total babe. A lot of women have tried to entice him into marriage, but since he lost his wife, he hasn't been interested." She shrugged, her gaze turning soft and a little dreamy. "I guess he must have really loved her. Rumor is that's why he agreed to an arranged marriage this time around. He can't have Jasmine, but he needs an heir. Oh, and of course, the Fortiers are rich. I'm guessing that helps."

Sarah set her glass down, suddenly losing any desire

for the drink or the conversation that had gone with it. The pipe dream that she could have a marriage, maybe even true and lasting love, with Gabe was receding fast. She had thought Nadia Fortier was the only problem but, according to the waitress, Nadia came in a bad second because he was still in love with a first wife that he'd almost never mentioned!

Tired and on edge after the night flight from Paris, Gabe negotiated Zahir's main street traffic, his temper on a tight rein as he noted the displays of ribbons and strings of colored lights, and the congratulatory messages that were appearing despite the wedding date being weeks away. His phone vibrated. He took the call while he waited at a traffic light.

Xavier, who had been met by his wife when they'd landed, sounded weary. "An Italian tabloid has gotten hold of the story that you're supposed to be holed up in a *castello* in Tuscany with Nadia. What do you want me to do?"

"What we always do, nothing." With any luck the fact that he had openly spent two days in New York and the past week in Dubai would discredit the gossip. "Any luck getting hold of Sarah?"

"Same luck you had. She's not answering her phone. Tarik went around. She wasn't home."

The sense of unease that had gripped him when he hadn't been able to get hold of Sarah before the flight from Paris returned full force. He tensed at the thought that she might have had another fainting episode. Maybe the diabetes had worsened and she'd been admitted to the hospital. He had thought she was okay now that her

diet was under control. But it was always possible she
had suffered some other complication.

Suddenly the distance between them, a distance he
had thought he needed in order to control his own emotions—was a barrier he was no longer prepared to tol-
erate. As soon as he could locate Sarah, he would make
arrangements to have her fly out to Zahir. Jaw taut, he
instructed Xavier to keep trying to locate Sarah, including checking the hospitals.

A thought occurred. Sarah had told him the man
she'd dated the night she and Gabe met at the consulate, Southwell, had once broken into her house. It was
possible he'd come back to harass her again. "And check
on Southwell."

Even though Sarah had finished with him, Gabe
couldn't rule out the fact that Southwell might try to
make another move on Sarah. "One more thing, ask
Tarik to check the airport manifests just in case Sarah
has left the country."

Gabe hung up as the light changed. He inched forward in the heavy traffic. He was probably overreacting.
It was possible Sarah had gone away for a few days, although that didn't explain why she hadn't called or answered her phone. Wherever she was, she would still
have a cell phone, which meant she was choosing to be
out of contact with him.

He frowned at that thought. Usually, Sarah was more
than happy to talk for as long as he wanted to stay on
the phone. For her to close off all communication meant
something had happened. His fingers tightened on the
wheel. At a guess, she had picked up on the scandal
brewing around Nadia.

The fact that Sarah had reacted by closing him out,

the kind of manipulative tactic Jasmine had often used, should have had him backing off from the relationship. Instead, he thought grimly, it was having the opposite effect and for good reason. Even though he was certain Sarah was emotionally involved with him, she had also made it crystal clear that vulnerability was optional: she could get along without him.

Gabe braked as a truck pulled out from the curb and brooded on the prospect that Sarah might have made the kind of bold, declarative decision she seemed prone to make and ditched him. Caught in traffic, surrounded by the hubbub of a hot Zahiri day, Gerald Fortier's manipulation still leaving a bad taste, it was an odd moment for Gabe to reach a point of absolute clarity about the future.

He had made a mistake in leaving Sarah alone for so long. It was a mistake he would not make again. Now that he had terminated the agreement with Fortier, he was going to insist he and Sarah get engaged immediately.

Gabe had almost reached the palace when Xavier rang with the news that Sarah had left New Zealand and landed in Zahir that morning.

Fierce satisfaction curled through Gabe. Sarah hadn't run from him, she was here, on his island. And there could be only one reason: she had come after him.

She loved him, he was suddenly certain of it. Nothing else explained why she had let him make love to her in the first place and then been willing to take him back, even after he had left her flat.

The thought that Sarah was committed enough to come to Zahir in search of him should have sounded alarm bells, but the relief that she had done so somehow canceled out any recoil he should feel. He had dreaded Jasmine's brand of intense, cloying love, but he found he did not feel the same way about Sarah. If Sarah was in love with him then, as far as he was concerned, that provided a counterbalance to her strong will and a measure of certainty he needed. The desire to consolidate their relationship with marriage settled even more firmly into place. He registered that Xavier was still talking.

"Uh—as it happens Southwell is also on Zahir, but they're not staying at the same hotel and they didn't travel together."

Frowning at the irritating specter of Southwell, Gabe did a U-turn and headed for the hotel. He braked for a stream of pedestrians crossing to a waterfront souk. A woman dressed in white with dark, caramel-streaked hair arranged in a sexy knot caught his eye. He couldn't see her face, but something about the confident feminine stride spun him back to a stormy night in Wellington.

Traffic moved at a snail's pace as the woman in white paused at the entrance to the souk. Hitching the strap of her handbag a little higher on her shoulder, she checked her watch. Gabe's heart slammed against the wall of his chest. He would recognize the elegant shape of her cheekbones, the smoky slant of her eyes and that delicate, faintly imperious nose anywhere. It was Sarah.

There was no place to park on the congested street, so he backed up a few feet, waited on traffic then turned down a narrow lane that ran down one side of the souk. There was no official parking, just dedicated loading bays for the stallholders. He found a space at the back of a diamond merchant's shop and parked.

As he locked the car, the security guard for the merchant, a tall heavyset man dressed in a suit, stepped into the loading bay. His grim expression changed when he noted Gabe's signature kaffiyeh and *agal*. Moments later, the security guard was joined by the owner, who assured Gabe he could leave his car for as long as he wanted. The effusive offer was followed by a sales pitch on a line of diamond earrings that would make Gabe's future bride melt with desire.

Gabe assured the owner of the souk that if he required diamonds, he would be sure to consider him. It was a fact that now that the way was clear to marry Sarah, he would need a ring. It would seal the engagement and be a tangible sign that Sarah was his.

He found himself wondering what kind of diamond Sarah would like. It was not the kind of question that had ever consumed him before. Jasmine had insisted on choosing her own ring, and he had never known what Nadia liked; the ring she had received had been chosen by Hasim. But Gabe had an intimate knowledge of Sarah's tastes: fresh flowers and spicy food; old-fashioned, mismatched dinner plates; colorful, funky kids' clothes. *His* kid's clothes.

Stepping out into the main thoroughfare, Gabe skimmed the press of shoppers that flowed like colorful flotsam through the streets. Most were Western tourists, drawn here by a media campaign that had been formulated by Zahir's young and aggressive minister of tourism. A Harvard graduate Gabe had met while he was studying, Faruq Malik was intent on selling Zahir as an island of romance, history and mysticism.

Faruq had left no stone unturned in his attempt to resurrect the mystery of Camille's lost bridal dowry and the first Sheikh Kadin's ancient romance. He had even invented new aspects to the story, claiming that the moon had been full the night of the wedding and that the vows had been exchanged at midnight.

Gabe glimpsed a cool flash of white in a sea of vibrant reds, blues, oranges and glaring pinks. He made his way through eager streams of shoppers, all avid for gold and silks, jewel-bright rugs and exotic spices, until he reached the silk merchant's shop that Sarah had entered.

A group of Japanese tourists were clustered around the counter. Sarah half turned as he entered the shop, a sumptuous drift of berry-red silk held draped against her body. For a split second, Gabe was riveted. The sensual richness of the cloth seemed to make her skin glow and her eyes seem even darker and more exotic.

Red. It was her color.

Sarah's gaze passed blithely over him then zapped back. *"You."*

The fiery glare spun him back to the conversation in his Jeep when Sarah had discovered he had gotten engaged straight after they had made love. She had been angry and then she had kissed him.

A purely masculine satisfaction filled him. If Sarah had been disconnected and indifferent, he would be worried, but she wasn't. She was mad, her glare pointed and highly personal as if everything that was wrong was his fault. Which, if she had read the gutter-press story claiming that he was holed up with Nadia in Italy, was understandable.

In the heat of that glare, he found himself feeling oddly at home, as if they had just picked up on a half-finished conversation. In that moment he realized how much he'd missed the long phone calls and the electrical connection that seemed to hum between them. Crazily, putting distance between them had done nothing to lessen what he felt for her.

"Sarah. What a surprise to find you on Zahir."

Ten

Unwillingly arrested by the traditional kaffiyeh and *agal*, which had distracted her from recognizing that it was Gabe filling the shop doorway, Sarah dumped the red cloth back in a bin filled with colored silks. The low timbre of his voice shivered through her, but she refused to be seduced by it. Been there, done that, she thought grimly. Didn't want the T-shirt.

She dredged up a cool smile. "I'd hate to miss your wedding."

In the dim interior of the shop, dressed in a dark suit with the kaffiyeh, his jaw stubbled as if he hadn't had time to shave, his amber eyes gleaming in the shadows, he looked exotic and even larger and edgier than she remembered.

Her anger and hurt that he had not canceled his wedding and had spent the past couple of weeks at some

Italian *castello* with Nadia dropped to a slow simmer as Sarah registered how utterly out of place Gabe was in a silk merchant's shop. That could only mean that he had seen her and followed her into the shop. The thought instigated a flicker of pleasure that she could not allow to make headway, given that Gabe had betrayed both her and their baby and from all accounts had enjoyed every moment of it.

Her anger bolstered by that thought, she lifted her chin another notch and decided she had nothing to lose by the direct approach. "Where's Nadia?"

A deathly silence descended on the shop.

Gabe glanced at the number of women filling the shop. "We need to talk...elsewhere."

Dimly, Sarah realized there seemed to be a lot of women holding cell phones. Cell phones equaled photographs, social media, maybe even a video of the conversation. She imagined it was the kind of situation that had happened to him in Tuscany.

When she didn't immediately follow his order, Gabe gave her the kind of irritated look that made her feel like *she* had betrayed *him*. A split second later she found herself hustled out into blazing sunlight.

Gabe gave her a searing glance as he threaded his way through a stream of shoppers and into a shaded alleyway between merchants' shops. "I haven't been with Nadia. I've been in the Emirates negotiating with a building contractor for most of the past week. Finding cell phone coverage is difficult. Does that answer your question?"

She dug in her heels, halting them both and tried not to notice that with the snowy-white kaffiyeh framing the masculine planes of his face, Gabe looked almost fiercely beautiful and completely at home in the sun-drenched souk. "So that wasn't you at the *castello* in Tuscany?"

He said something curt beneath his breath. She was fairly certain it was one of his swear words. "Since I've never been to Tuscany, no, it wasn't."

He hadn't been with Nadia. Relief surged through Sarah, making her feel faintly dizzy. Silly, emotional tears pricked at the backs of her eyes.

Blinking furiously, she searched in her bag and found a tissue. "Who was it, then?"

"Raoul Fabrizio. Some Italian count." Gabe ducked down and peered into her eyes. "Damn, you're crying."

As she dabbed her eyes and blew her nose, she found herself eased into a loose embrace. The deep rumble of his voice and the steady thud of his heart were oddly soothing. She drew a shallow breath, and the clean scent of his skin laced with the irresistible whiff of sandal-wood that she had worked so hard to forget made her tense. After days of stress and fury it was hard to adjust to the fact that he wasn't the villain she'd been building up in her mind.

Sniffing, she blew her nose again. "I never cry. It must be the pregnancy."

When she searched for a second tissue, he handed her a beautifully folded handkerchief. "How have you been? Have you put on weight?"

She stared at the monogramed handkerchief, which was too beautiful to use, and tried not to be seduced by the deep, velvety timbre of his voice. She glared at him. "Do you really care?"

A couple of tourists strolling in the direction of the beach, towels slung over their shoulders, glanced at them curiously.

Gabe frowned. "We can't talk here. If you'll come with me now, I know a place where we can be private."

Sarah checked her wristwatch and tried to look like she was on a schedule and wasn't quite sure if she could fit Gabe in. "Will it take long?"

"You've got other appointments?"

A fresh wave of hurt and anger fountained up at the note of incredulity in Gabe's voice, as if pregnant, abandoned history teachers did not have appointments. "I'm not on Zahir for a holiday. Now that I've got a child to support, I'm starting a new career as a travel writer."

His brows jerked together. "You don't need a job. I'll support you and the baby."

She pulled free of his hold, fire shooting from her eyes. "I will not be dependent on you."

"I didn't ask you to be."

The calm timbre of his voice somehow defused the anger that kept trying to erupt, conversely leaving her feeling vulnerable and unsure. Sarah decided she preferred the anger.

Gabe indicated they should follow the couple with the towels. Aware of him close behind her, a few steps later Sarah found herself in a service lane lined with vans and small trucks.

The sidelights of a sleek black sedan with darkly tinted windows flashed as Gabe unlocked the vehicle. Sarah stopped in her tracks. "You said we would talk somewhere in private, not that you wanted to put me in a car and drive me somewhere."

He looked momentarily arrested as he held the passenger-side door. "It's not that sinister. All I want to do is find somewhere private to talk where we won't be overheard. I've got a beach house five minutes away. If you don't want to go there, we could go to your hotel."

Her eyes widened. "You know where I'm staying?"

Frustration burned in his gaze. "Zahir's not exactly a big country—"

"So you sicced some kind of Zahiri secret service on me."

"It wasn't that high-tech. Xavier called the airport."

Sarah climbed into the luxurious Audi and tried not to like the chill of air-conditioned air and the smell of new leather. "Your henchman. I should have known."

Gabe closed the door then walked around and slid behind the wheel. "Xavier's not a henchman. We decided not to have those a few years back. He's head of palace security. Mostly he checks locks and alarm systems. Occasionally he checks out people who are close to the family."

She fastened her seat belt and tried not to love the sexy quirk to Gabe's mouth as he took off the *kaffiyeh* and *agal* and tossed them on the backseat. Instead she needed to remember how easy he found it to forget about her.

His comment about people close to the family got her attention. "But your family doesn't actually know about me."

His gaze dropped to her mouth, making her heart pound. "Of course they know about you and the baby."

Feeling mollified and altogether calmer now that she knew he had actually told his parents about her, she relaxed back into the cloud-like seat. Deliciously cool air washed over her as Gabe accelerated into traffic. He stopped for a stream of pedestrians heading for the souks and Sarah stiffened as her cell phone chimed. Aware of

Gabe's proximity and that he would hear every word she spoke, she picked up the call from her mother.

The conversation was brief. Hannah wanted to know how Sarah was and if she'd checked into her hotel. She also wanted to let her know that she had heard from a mutual acquaintance that Graham was on Zahir.

Sarah frowned at the mention of Graham, who must still be on his wild-goose hunt for the missing dowry. After their last meeting when he had broken into her home, she had no interest in seeing him ever again. Luckily, with all the holidaymakers on Zahir, the chances that she and Graham would actually cross paths were slim.

Gabe turned down a narrow driveway that flowed beneath a shady grove of ancient olives. He brought the car to a halt outside a villa built on a small rise overlooking a tiny, jewel-like bay. "Was that Southwell?"

Sarah grasped the door handle. It would be a simple matter to say it was her mother, but after the past week of turmoil and uncertainty, she still felt ruffled and hurt. "I don't think that's any of your business."

Leaning across, he pulled the door shut, trapping her in place. "I don't want you seeing Southwell."

For a moment she was close enough that she could see the faint shadows under his eyes, as if he hadn't gotten a lot of sleep, and the intriguing roughness of his five-o'clock shadow. "I wouldn't see Graham Southwell if he was the last man on earth."

He let go of his hold on the door. "Who were you talking to, then?"

She wanted to stick to her resolve to leave Gabe in the dark about her personal life, and let him experience a little uncertainty. But with Gabe close enough that she could feel the heat blasting off his body and breathe in his clean masculine scent it was difficult to think straight. Unfortunately, she was also seduced by the dizzying notion that Gabe was jealous. If he was jealous, that meant he did care for her. "It was my mother."

His gaze dropped to her mouth, sending a sharp tingle of heat through her. "My apologies," he said curtly. "But I was worried about you. Southwell is on Zahir, too."

She tried not to stare into his irises, which really were a mesmerizing hue of amber, striped with chocolate brown. "Graham comes here a lot. Besides being an importer, he's obsessed with finding Camille's dowry."

He *was* jealous. A dizzying surge of pleasure flowed through her, warming her from the inside out so that she was practically purring. "Did Xavier make a call to find out where Graham is?"

Gabe's gaze narrowed, signaling that she was playing with fire, but she didn't care. As wary as she was about what he might feel for her, she loved him. He was the father of her child and he'd been gone for over two weeks, and in that time she had *missed* him. Added to that, she had thought she was on the brink of losing him to a woman she was certain he did not love. As far as she was concerned she had a right to the truth.

"To be strictly accurate, Xavier asked an investigative firm to confirm Southwell's movements."

But Gabe had paid for the report. She had to suppress the sappy desire to grin. "Isn't that a bit paranoid?"

"Not from where I'm standing. I needed to know that he wouldn't come near you."

He *was* jealous.

Feeling suddenly giddy that not only had Gabe not slept with Nadia, but that in the time he'd been absent, he had actually worried about her, she pushed the door wide and stepped out onto a pristine white shell drive.

Gabe gestured at a path that led to a shady patio overlooking the sea. He unlocked and opened a set of French doors. She stepped into a sitting room shaded by shutters. Tiled floors were strewn with bright Zahiri rugs and low, comfortable couches were strategically placed to make the most of the stunning view.

Gabe walked through to a sleek kitchen that opened off the sitting room. "Would you like a drink?"

The polite request distracted her from checking out the beautiful house that was obviously not Gabe's primary residence since it had been shut up for some time. "Water will be fine."

She heard the opening of the refrigerator, the chink of ice. Gabe indicated she should take a seat. When she did so, she found herself staring at a vivid oil painting of a woman seated in an enclosed garden, wearing a vivid flame red dress.

"Camille." Gabe handed Sarah a frosted glass then strolled to the open doors to stare out at the view.

Gaze drawn to the broad width of his shoulders emphasized by the snug fit of his suit jacket, Sarah sipped a mouthful of water. Unable to bear the silence, she asked, "What did you want to talk about?"

He turned, his expression oddly neutral. "Us. As of last night I'm no longer obligated to marry Nadia. I'm proposing that we should get married next month."

Eleven

For long moments, Sarah thought she had heard wrong. She set her glass down on the beautiful ebony table, careful not to spill any water on what looked like a precious antique. "You really mean it, you want to marry me?"

Gabe's expression was still curiously neutral. She realized the descriptive she should be using was "guarded."

Given his worry over Graham, she knew Gabe had feelings for her. But she was also aware that his approach to marriage was just a little too businesslike. He hadn't said he loved her, and he very probably didn't at this stage. Her stomach dipped when she realized he almost never mentioned his first wife.

The reality was that for now the pregnancy was dictating what happened next, but Sarah had hoped for something more, a glimpse of the warmth and love they could share once they were living together.

Despite her efforts to stay just as guarded as he, her heart swelled with emotion. The problem was, she thought a little desperately, that she loved him and she wanted to marry him—even if he didn't feel the same right now. "Next month?"

He mentioned a date and her stomach plunged. She knew that date. It was engraved in fiery letters on her heart. Despite her effort to stay calm, she found herself on her feet, too upset to sit. "I presume you mean the same date you were going to marry Nadia?"

"Yes."

The cautious joy that he did still want to marry her was swamped by annoyance. "Let me guess, the wedding venue is booked, the guests are invited and there's no wedding without a bride?" She knew how that went, since she'd had to cancel wedding plans, twice.

"I know it's not ideal, but it's a fact that we need to get married soon, and the wedding, which is important for Zahir, has been arranged."

"I understand the practicalities." But it was hard to feel cherished and special when the proposal sounded as forced as Gabe's last engagement, and when she was being offered a second-hand wedding.

Still caught in the curious ambivalence of receiving the proposal she wanted from Gabe but in a way that sounded more like a transaction than a relationship, Sarah paced to the portrait of Camille.

A small heated tingle shot down her spine as she registered Gabe close behind her. Determined to control her response to him, she concentrated on the painting. "She had style."

"She was a woman who knew what she wanted."

Sarah couldn't help wondering if that was how Gabe

viewed her. "Is there anything wrong with knowing what you want?"

"Not as long as it means you'll say yes and marry me."

She swung around, his words sending a bittersweet pang through her. She had thought he hadn't noticed that she hadn't actually agreed to marry him yet. They had made plans back in New Zealand, but all of that had been tentative, knowing he had to end things with Nadia first.

Sarah wanted marriage, but only because she truly believed he might fall for her over time. She guessed she had hoped he might view their relationship as more than just a solution. "Do you want to marry me?"

His expression closed up and she wondered if she'd said something wrong, then his hands curved around her upper arms, seductively warm against her skin.

"We're good together. We like one another. We're going to have a child."

And the lovemaking had been off the register. Two weeks ago it had seemed almost enough. "What about the money?"

"Money is no longer an issue for Zahir." Gabe's fingers meshed with her's, pulling her close. "I want you, Sarah, and I think you know that. I have spent weeks making and breaking deals to have you. Will you marry me?"

Time seemed to slow, stop. She had wanted to change her life, to take risks, and she had. Now there was no way she could go back to the flat and endless routine of her old life. This version of life might be hurtful, but at least she knew she was alive.

Above all, she had to think about the baby. If there was a chance for them to be a real family, she had to take it. "Yes."

Relief flared in his gaze. He bent and touched his mouth to hers.

The slow, lingering kiss sent a hot pang all the way to her toes. Before she could stop herself, she clutched his shoulders, lifted up and deepened the kiss. This was what she had wanted, what she had longed for even when trying to be cautious.

Gabe's arms closed around her, fitting her even more closely against him. Relief flooded her as she felt the firm shape of his arousal pressing against her hip. His blunt, masculine response was a reassurance that, in the wake of the article claiming that he was with Nadia, she badly needed.

When he lifted his head, she boldly wound her arms around his neck and instigated another lingering kiss. When Gabe dragged pins from her hair so that it cascaded around her shoulders then lifted her against him so that her feet left the ground, the eroticism of it sent a flush of heat through her.

When he lowered her to the floor, she felt the cool leather of a couch at the backs of her knees. With a tingle of excitement, she realized he had carried her there while they'd kissed.

He tangled his fingers in her hair, his gaze burned into hers. "Are you well enough to make love?"

Heat burned through her at the question. "I'm fine, never better."

He kissed her again. They were going to make love. The reality of it, when an hour ago she was in the depths of despair, was faintly shocking.

With fingers that fumbled slightly, she unknotted his silk tie then started on the buttons of his shirt. Irresistible flashes of the last time they'd made love kept making her heart pound out of control. There were a lot of things about their relationship that needed working on, but she couldn't help thinking that this part was absolutely perfect.

Minutes later, with her dress lying puddled on the floor, Gabe lowered her to the leather couch. He had already dispensed with his jacket and shirt, and now eased out of his pants. As he tossed stretchy gray boxers on the floor, she drank in the sight of him, naked. In her bedroom, at night, he had been beautiful. In full daylight, the hot Zahiri sunlight making him look bronzed and sleek and muscular, he was breathtaking.

He joined her on the couch, his weight pressing her down. Automatically, she moved to accommodate him. His gaze locked with hers and a faint tension assailed her as she felt him lodged against her. Now that marriage and a baby were part of their equation, she was worried that she might disappoint him in some way. After all, she was not a glamorous jet-setter like Nadia, or a fragile beauty like his first wife.

A split second later the worry ceased to be important as she held her breath against the exquisite moment of their joining. He kissed her then pulled her closer still, holding her tight against him as if he needed her, as if she truly mattered to him, as they moved together and the afternoon dissolved in a blinding shimmer of heat.

Much later, after they'd both showered and dressed, Gabe found his cell and pressed a speed dial. "Hasim will take care of the change to the invitations. Meantime, I'll need you to stay on in your hotel and keep our engagement under wraps until the palace issues a press release."

Still caught in the rosy aftermath of lovemaking, the

sudden switch to the "business" of the wedding was a little jarring. Sarah picked up her handbag and adjusted the strap over one shoulder. "Stay in the hotel, as in lay low?"

Gabe's gaze settled on her mouth and lingered. Not quite all business, then, she thought with relief.

"It would be expedient. Once the press get hold of this they'll go crazy—"

Whoever Gabe was calling picked up. He half turned away while he spoke in rapid Zahiri. A few minutes later, he hung up and slipped the phone back in his shirt pocket. "That was Faruq, the minister of tourism. He'll take care of the press release. Once the announcement is made, we can move you into the palace."

Gabe drove Sarah back to her hotel, taking the time to question her about her and the baby's health, wanting verbatim accounts of exactly what Evelyn had said. Sarah couldn't help basking in his concern. To her mind, like the beautiful, off-the-register lovemaking, it was a sign that he was falling for her.

Feeling bemused and a little dreamy after the hours they'd spent making love, Sarah strolled into the deep shade of the hotel's portico. Graham's sudden appearance as he popped up from a café table caught her completely off guard.

His gaze swept her with that hint of disbelief she still found irritating. As if updating her look had somehow changed her beyond all recognition. Still intensely annoyed with Graham for breaking into her house and copying the journal, she fixed him with a flat glare. "What do you want?"

"Do I have to want something?"

When he opened his arms as if they were actually going to hug, Sarah stepped back, neatly avoiding the fake intimacy. "In my experience, yes. Although I thought you'd already gotten what you wanted."

Unfazed, Graham fell into step beside her as she strolled into the gorgeous mosaic tile lobby.

"Mostly. I think I'm finally onto something, I just need you to decipher the piece of the journal that's still written in Old French—"

"No." Sarah stepped into an elevator. As the doors slid closed, Graham's expression was red-faced and belligerent, but she didn't care. She was too absorbed with Gabe to pay attention to Graham.

The elevator doors opened on her floor and she found herself staring blankly at a pair of probable honeymooners, their eyes starry, skin tanned, bright new wedding rings gleaming on their fingers.

As she strolled to her suite, she checked her watch, dazed at how little time had passed. Just over three hours since she had left. And yet in that time Gabe had found her, proved their attraction was still fiery and tingling with life. They had made love and the engagement had been confirmed.

Pulse speeding up at the memory of their lovemaking, she stepped into her suite and caught a glimpse of her reflection in the mirror by the door. She touched a red mark on the side of her neck. She remembered Gabe's jaw scraping her tender skin, the ripple of sensation that had gone through her at the utterly sensual caress, as if he couldn't get enough of her.

She drew a deep breath as it sank in just how much she had changed.

She was no longer the dry, low-key history teacher who had stayed in Friday, Saturday...let's face it, *every night*. She was the kind of risk-taking woman who attracted a sheikh and who, after one wildly passionate night, was carrying his child.

Gabe had made love to her as if she was desirable, as if he couldn't resist her. As if she belonged to him.

Just as she knew that Gabe was hers.

A little startled by the clear, bold thought, she set her bag down and strolled to the refrigerator to get herself a cold drink. Carrying the ice water back to the sitting room, she sat down on the sofa and booted up her tablet. After the conversation with the waitress in the café, she was even more curious about Gabe's first marriage. Maybe she should have asked him about it, but she hadn't quite been able to broach the subject because she had wanted him to confide in her.

Minutes later, she had turned up an old tabloid report that seemed to confirm everything she'd heard. Gabe and Jasmine had been childhood sweethearts and married young. She had died tragically in a boating accident.

Another search turned up a series of photographs of Jasmine, fragile and breathtakingly pretty, an enormous diamond solitaire sparkled on her finger.

A ring. It was a small detail and something Sarah and Gabe hadn't spoken about, something they hadn't had time for, yet.

The phone rang. When Graham's voice registered, she slammed the receiver down then took the phone off the hook. For good measure she also turned her cell off then went back to her tablet.

A couple of hours later, a rap on the door woke her from a nap. She checked the peephole in case it was Graham. It was Gabe.

Still feeling on edge about Gabe's almost complete

silence about his first wife, she opened the door. Gabe was obviously freshly showered and looked utterly gorgeous in dark pants and a light, gauzy shirt. "I didn't expect to see you so soon."

His gaze narrowed as he picked up on the coolness in her voice. "I tried to ring but your cell seems to be turned off, and the hotel phone is off the hook. There's been a change of plan. I've arranged a house for you to move into. It was originally a fortress, so it's more secure than the hotel. If you can collect your things I'll take you out now, then I thought we might go out for dinner."

She stiffened at the calm way he was making arrangements, as if he'd smoothly moved past the minor glitch of almost losing her. Before she could stop herself, the question she'd promised herself she would not ask burst out of her. "Why don't you ever talk about your first wife?"

His expression turned bleak. "The marriage ended years ago."

Her fingers tightened on the doorknob. "But you haven't forgotten her."

"My wife died, that's not something I'm likely to forget."

Instantly, she felt guilty and contrite that she'd stirred up painful memories. Although that didn't stop her wondering if the reason Gabe wasn't falling for her was because he was still in love with his dead wife.

A group of cleaners, one pushing a trolley filled with cleaning products, strolled past, their expressions openly curious.

Gabe kept his gaze firmly fixed on her. "Why did you turn your phones off?"

Her brows jerked together at the probing question. She had only had her phones off for a couple of hours, while Gabe had been incommunicado for a whole week. "I bumped into Graham in the foyer. He tried to follow me to my room, then he started calling."

"Southwell." Gabe straightened, a grim fire burning in his gaze. "That's why I've arranged the shift to the old fortress."

He glanced at the cleaners who had stopped a short distance away and who seemed fascinated by their conversation. "We can't discuss this in the corridor. Are you going to let me in?"

A little thrill shooting down her spine, she stepped back as Gabe stalked into her suite.

Closing the door, he crossed his arms over his chest. "What did Southwell want?"

"He wanted me to translate some Old French from the journal."

Gabe looked briefly arrested. "You know Old French?"

"I did a couple of papers in historical linguistics." She shrugged. "I'm not as good as Laine."

He shook his head, the grimness morphing into an expression that made her heart race, as if he liked her quirky, oddball education, more, as if he liked *her*.

He shook his head slightly. "Damn," he muttered. "Back to Southwell. If he ever comes near you again, call me immediately. And if you're thinking of arguing about the move out to the house, you can forget it. I need you safe."

Another small thrill shot down her spine at the flat series of commands, most especially the last statement, that Gabe needed her safe, as if her safety was personally important to him. And in that moment she knew that Gabe's feelings toward her were neither neutral nor businesslike.

She had a sudden flashback to the night of the cocktail party at the Zahiri consulate, the moment when Gabe had walked out of the stormy night to rescue her.

The gloom that had enshrouded her when she had been focused on Gabe's wife, Jasmine, dissipated. She had been concentrating on the past, but what was happening right now was significant. Gabe had gone out on a limb for her. He had changed his country's constitution, brokered deals and canceled his marriage contract. He wanted her—enough that he'd made her pregnant. Now he wanted to put her in a fortress to keep her safe.

They were not the actions of a businessman wanting a marriage of convenience; they were the actions of a warrior with a passionate heart. A heart that had *not* been buried with his wife.

Twelve

The drive out to the house, which was situated on a cliff above Salamander Bay, took fifteen minutes along a narrow, winding road. The house itself stole Sarah's breath, because although it had been extensively remodeled it was clear that the original structure had once been a cliff-top fortress.

Gabe introduced her to the resident housekeeper and gardener, Marie and Carlos.

She chose a room that had white walls and dark floorboards strewn with jewel-bright rugs, and which contained a huge four-poster bed draped with a filmy mosquito net. Light and airy French doors opened onto a stone balcony, and like many of the rooms she'd glimpsed, there was a spectacular view of the sea.

Sarah quickly unpacked then dressed for dinner in a softly draped red chiffon dress that floated off her shoulders and clung in all the right places. When she walked downstairs, Gabe strolled in from the terrace, which opened off a large sitting room that seemed filled with antique furniture and artwork.

Her interest piqued, she examined the carving on a chest that inhabited one corner of the room. "This must be a twelfth-century piece if it's a day. Looks like it came off a ship."

"It came off Camille's ship, the *Salamander*. It's one of the few objects that survived the wreck." He nodded in the direction of the terrace. "If you want to see the remains of the *Salamander*, the outline of the hull, which is mostly buried, is still visible."

Sarah followed Gabe out onto the windswept terrace.

Gabe leaned on the parapet, as he pointed out the shadowy outline of her ancestor's ship, still visible where it had foundered in the rocky shallows of Salamander Bay.

Once she had seen the wreck, he hurried her back inside. "We need to discuss meeting my parents and we need to do it fast, because they're on their way here."

The sharp chiming of the doorbell sounded in the distance.

Gabe's expression turned rueful. "Too late. They've already arrived."

Moments later Sarah heard the click of high heels on ancient flagstones as Maria showed the Sheikh of Zahir and Gabe's mother into the great room.

The sheikh was tall and lean with a dark, penetrating gaze. Forty years on, Gabe would look exactly like him. Gabe's mother was slim and medium height. Despite being in her fifties, with her dark blond hair smoothed into a stylish short cut, she looked a good ten years younger than her husband.

The instant Hilary Kadir saw Sarah her face softened, and Sarah knew it was going to be all right.

Hilary gave Sarah a hug. "Your name's Sarah?" Sarah barely had time to nod before Hilary continued. "Are you all right? Is he treating you okay?" She shot Gabe a faintly accusing look then smiled apologetically before introducing herself and her husband.

The sheikh was kind, but formal. From the paleness of his skin, Sarah guessed he was still unwell, so she hurried to offer him a seat then blushed because she'd been here less than an hour, and the house belonged to the Kadir family.

Hilary smiled. "We're sorry for the ambush, but when I heard you were pregnant I couldn't stay away. Since Jasmine—"

"Mom."

Hilary frowned at Gabe and sent Sarah an apologetic look. "If we'd known there was a baby, we would have been in contact a whole lot sooner."

Marie arrived with a tea tray.

Broodingly, Gabe watched as Sarah fielded his mother's questions. Until that moment he hadn't realized how on edge he had been about this particular meeting.

The turnaround in his thinking was immense and complete. He had gone from an organized, convenient marriage to marrying a woman he wanted. It was the exact opposite of the situation he had planned.

Gabe's father was understandably cautious about the relationship, even with a baby on the way. Gabe knew that the biggest obstacle for his father right now was accepting the money situation, but he had finally handed the financial reins over to Gabe with his blessing.

His gaze rested on Sarah as she talked with his mother, who was a talented linguist. Whimsically, he wondered what his mother would think when she found out that, like her, Sarah could read Old French. Sarah reached up and adjusted a pin in her hair, and the memory of what it had felt like to have those strands cascade over his hands in a silky mass made him tense.

Dispassionately, he examined why he was so attracted to Sarah. Possibly it was because, with her double degree and forthright manner, she was as unlike Jasmine as it was possible to be. Although that wasn't the whole of it, and the way he reacted to Southwell was a case in point.

Gabe considered the thought that he was jealous and dismissed it. Sarah was pregnant with his child, she was going to be his wife and Southwell was an unsavory character. There would be something wrong with him if he didn't react possessively.

Hilary smiled at Sarah, her gaze narrowed shrewdly as she and her husband got ready to leave. "You love him, don't you? I can tell."

Sarah felt heat rise up in her cheeks. "Yes."

She let out a breath, gripped by the thought that it was really that simple. She loved Gabe and she had from the first. A lot of things had happened that should have killed that love, but through all the reversals and the stinging betrayal of finding out he was engaged to Nadia, she hadn't let go. Somehow her emotions were stubbornly anchored. She couldn't imagine losing interest in Gabe; everything about him fascinated and drew her. She even loved his occasional bad temper because when it came down to it she would rather fight with Gabe than spend time with anyone else.

Although she had to be careful not to let him know that.

"He likes you," Hilary said quietly. "And I think he's over the moon that you're pregnant. A lot of marriages have started with less."

Gabe took Sarah to a small restaurant down on the waterfront, which had a private room. Seated on a balcony right over the water, the setting couldn't have been more romantic. Although the dinner had a practical aspect. While they ate, Gabe filled her in on more family information, including the names of about twenty cousins, most of them female, and a raft of children.

"After meeting my mother you'll understand why you need to know this stuff. She's big on family."

"I like your mother." They'd chatted for ages, and Sarah had hemorrhaged most of her life story, including the two failed engagements. As appalled as she'd been over spilling those kinds of details, in the end she hadn't minded because there had been a genuinely compassionate streak to Hilary Kadir.

After dinner, Gabe took her for a walk along the waterfront. The romanticism of the moonlit walk was somewhat marred by the fact that a very large bodyguard trailed them all the way.

She glanced at the guard, who was trying to look inconspicuous, but at six feet eight inches, with huge shoulders, that was difficult. "Do you always have a bodyguard?" Offhand she couldn't remember seeing one in New Zealand.

Gabe looped his arm around her shoulders, drawing her close. "It depends. Sometimes I slip the leash."

Half an hour later, Gabe dropped her off at the fortress house. He hadn't suggested they sleep together, which had been obsessing her through the evening, because after what had happened at the beach house that afternoon she had assumed they would continue to sleep together. When his fingers tangled with hers when she opened the door, relief made her feel a little shaky and she found herself inviting him in.

The house was dark except for a couple of lamps left burning in the sitting room. Sarah automatically gravitated to the balcony, with its view. Gabe's arms came around her and it seemed the most natural thing in the world to turn and kiss him. Long minutes later, he pulled her inside with him.

The perfumed warmth of the night air flowed around them as they undressed in her room. Somehow the more leisurely pace, so different from the fierce interlude in the beach house that afternoon, seemed even more intimate. Breathlessly she realized that this time they had all night.

With easy strength, Gabe swung her into his arms, lowered her to the bed and came down beside her. He cupped the small mound of her stomach then one rounded breast and she logged his curiosity.

"These are different."

"They changed almost immediately."

He bent his head and kissed each breast. The sensations low in her stomach coiled, tightened.

He lifted his head. "Do you want me to use a condom?"

The roughness of his voice and the jolting practicality of his question registered, but somehow couldn't mar the magic of the night. He hadn't asked the question when they'd made love earlier. She ran her hand down his chest, loving the heated feel of his skin. "Why use one when we don't need it?"

He went very still. "Are you sure?"

Her breath suddenly locked in her throat. "Unless there's a reason that you should use one."

"There isn't. I haven't been with anyone since you."

Out of nowhere joy hit her. His words weren't a declaration of love, but they were significant. She touched the scar on his cheekbone, running the tips of her fingers gently across the smooth tissue. He captured her hand, deliberately possessive as he bent and kissed her again. She clutched at Gabe's shoulders, drawing him close, lifting against him. This time their lovemaking was quieter, deeper, and as the night slowly unraveled around them she felt that something precious and right had flared to life between them.

She woke to gray morning light and the sound of Gabe in her shower. He dressed in the clothing he'd worn the previous night and dropped a kiss on her cheek. Since he didn't have any clothes at the house he had to return to his apartment at the palace to change. Feeling sleepy and bemused, Sarah agreed to meet him for lunch.

Gabe made a quick call to the guard who had looked after them last night, arranging for him to pick her up around eleven.

After Gabe had gone, Sarah had a leisurely breakfast out on the terrace then checked the palace's events online, noting that there was an open day today. It was part of the tourism promotion around the wedding, so

FIONA BRAND   149

the palace was bound to be crowded. Some spin doctor
called Faruq seemed to be running everything.

Since it was now supposed to be her wedding, she decided to take a risk and join a tour, despite Gabe's warning to stay out of sight for now. A tour of the palace as
an anonymous tourist would fill in time before lunch,
and provide more background information about Gabe's
family before she became an official part of it.

After changing into an ice-blue dress that looked fabulous with her new tan and a pair of sexy heels that were
comfortable for walking she strolled downstairs, talked
to Maria about the car in the garage and managed to
get the keys.

The sun burned down on the acres of perfectly man-
icured grounds and the elaborate wings and towers of
the palace. The building itself was impossibly beautiful
and romantic. To imagine that she would live there one
day soon seemed a dream.

Humming beneath her breath, Sarah took the tour,
journal in hand. Despite seeing photos, the palace took
her breath away with its vaulted ceilings, marble col-
umns and mosaic floors. Most of the tour seemed concentrated in the reception rooms that would be used for
the wedding, and those rooms were filled with a buzz of
activity as exquisite furniture was polished, fresh paint
applied to paneling and the gilding on the high, ornately
plastered ceilings was retouched.

As she lingered in a hallway that resembled an art
gallery, a slender young woman, accompanied by two
large men in suits with the unmistakable look of bodyguards, strolled by.

Shock reverberated through Sarah as she recognized

Nadia. With her hair trailing in loose, sexy tendrils, a gold-and-diamond pendant hanging suspended in the faint shadow of her cleavage, her wrists coiled with elegant bracelets, she looked more like a fashion model than the young heiress portrayed in her engagement photo.

Sarah's stomach lurched. There could only be one reason for her to be here; Nadia was trying to get Gabe back.

After all Sarah and Gabe had shared yesterday and last night, she shouldn't worry about Nadia's machinations. Yet she couldn't help but wonder—was this why Gabe hadn't wanted Sarah to come to the palace?

Thirteen

Frowning, Sarah watched where Nadia went as the tour trailed into a formal library that was in use by the family. Sarah glanced into a room that opened off the library and caught a glimpse of a familiar set of broad shoulders.

A small shock went through her. She hadn't expected to see Gabe. He had told her he would be in meetings all morning. Although of course, he hadn't said with *whom* he was meeting. Adrenaline zinged through her as Nadia strolled into view and it became obvious that Gabe was meeting with his ex-fiancée. In that moment the door to what must be Gabe's office closed, blocking Sarah's view.

Feeling ruffled and upset, because she had thought Nadia was out of the picture completely, she found herself marching toward the closed door. Popping it open, she breezed inside as if she was expected.

Gabe, who was leaning against a gleaming mahogany desk, turned his head, his gaze clashing with hers. Nadia stared at Sarah, clearly annoyed at the interruption.

Sarah plastered a steely smile on her face and kept her gaze on Gabe. "Darling, I hope I'm not interrupting anything important. I just wanted to check what time we were going to buy the engagement ring, before lunch or after?"

Marching up to Gabe, who looked taut and sleekly urban in a dark suit and pristine white shirt, a royal-blue tie at his throat, she went up on her toes. Curling her fingers into the lapels of his jacket, she kissed him on the mouth, noting the glint of amusement in his gaze.

His arm curled around her waist, holding her close. "How about before lunch?"

"Good, I'll just go and finish the…research I was doing next door." Kissing him one more time for good measure, Sarah made a beeline for the door.

Gabe's voice stopped her in her tracks. "How long will the research take?"

"I'll be researching until you're finished in here."

"That's what I thought."

Nadia started speaking in low, rapid French. Sarah, who spoke French fluently, understood fighting words when she heard them, then the door swung closed behind her, cutting off Gabe's reply.

Adrenaline pumping, Sarah walked straight into the tour group again, but she was no longer interested in the architectural and interior wonders of the palace. Peeling off, she practically jogged through the large library toward a set of French doors that opened onto a courtyard. Since the library was next to Gabe's office, if she walked outside, she should be able to hear what was going on between him and Nadia.

Tiptoeing over the paved courtyard outside, she sidled through a thick tropical shrub and peered into Gabe's office. Frustrated when she couldn't see anything, and wondering if somehow she had gotten the wrong office, she circumnavigated a tub of flowers and a trellis festooned with a dark, glossy creeper, to peer into the window.

"See anything interesting?"

The rough timbre of Gabe's voice spun Sarah around. When the heel of one shoe caught in the gap between pavers, she grabbed at a bunch of foliage to keep herself upright. "Not yet."

Gabe pulled her out of the shrubbery and picked a leaf out of her hair. "I thought we agreed you wouldn't come to the palace—"

"Because I'd find out you're meeting with your fiancée?"

"Ex-fiancée."

Sarah extracted herself from his hold. "It didn't look that way a few minutes ago."

"What you just saw was Gerald Fortier sending his daughter in to apply pressure. Apparently, he thought if I received a little 'encouragement' and an extra financial carrot, I'd go ahead with the marriage."

She stared at Gabe's stubbled jaw and an intriguing mark on the side of his neck. She could feel herself blushing at the memory of just how he had gotten that mark. "And were you encouraged?"

He cupped her nape, drawing her close. Dipping his head, he touched his mouth to hers, the kiss tingling all the way to her toes. He lifted his head. "If I was 'encouraged' do you think I'd be out here with you?"

She clutched at the lapels of his jacket again, using them as a convenient anchor. "I'm not going to apologize for making a scene." She had lost her last fiancée to another woman; she would not risk losing Gabe.

"Nadia Fortier's gone. Xavier's taken her back to her hotel. He's putting her on a chartered flight back to Paris this afternoon."

Gabe ushered her back through the library and into his office. "Now that you're here, I have something for you. I was going to give it to you at lunch, but with the damage Fortier's caused with leaked photos and documents, it needs to happen now. Faruq has set up a press conference straight after lunch, and I'd like you to attend it with me."

"You're going to officially announce our engagement?"

Gabe opened a wall safe and extracted a set of keys. In succinct tones he outlined the information that would be given to the media. In light of the fact that both he and Nadia had discovered they were not as compatible as they had first thought, they had ended their engagement. But, after the deepening of a relationship with a previous flame, a descendent of the de Vallois family, the wedding would proceed, just with a different bride. "We won't announce the pregnancy straight off. We can do that a few days before the wedding."

Sarah stiffened at the sanitized version of how the whole tangled situation had unfolded. There was nothing untruthful in the statement, but it was definitely constructed to distract attention away from the more scandalous aspects of the story.

Indicating that she should precede him, Sarah stepped out into the beautiful, echoing hall. Closing the door behind him, Gabe's hand dropped to the small of her back. A small tingle of pleasure went through her at his casual possessiveness as they strolled past tourists and palace staff who now stared at her with open curiosity.

A man in a suit acknowledged Gabe with a lift of his hand and fell into step behind them and the reality of her situation struck home. As Gabe's wife she would have to get used to security.

Gabe opened a heavy wooden slab of a door and they descended an ancient stone stairwell, leaving the brightness of day for the hard glow of artificial lighting. The dry coolness grew, enough to raise gooseflesh on her arms.

Gabe glanced at her, shrugged out of his jacket and dropped it around her shoulders. "I forget how cold it gets down here."

The jacket instantly swamped her with heat, sending a reflexive shiver through her. They stopped at another door, this one smaller in size and alarmed.

When Gabe had disarmed the door, she followed him into a room that had probably once been a cellar. He halted at a steel door that was utterly twenty-first century high-tech, unmistakably a vault, and tapped in a code. Depressing the handle, he pushed open the thick door.

The small room was lit with halogen bulbs and lined with metal shelves containing glass-fronted cabinets filled with ancient books, scrolls and archives that instantly piqued Sarah's interest. As an historian she loved examining original documents, although she seldom got the chance since most ancient texts were too fragile to be handled. There was also a series of locked steel cabinets and boxes. "Is this where the dowry used to be kept?"

Gabe checked through the ring of keys and found the one he wanted. "It was kept here, but in those days the security was primitive, just two locked doors and old-fashioned iron keys, which was why the dowry needed moving when the island was evacuated."

Gabe chose a cabinet, unlocked it then withdrew two midnight blue velvet cases. Setting them down on a sleek metal table that occupied the center of the vault, he opened the smallest. Already prepared for the fact that he was probably going to give her a ring because they were in the palace vault and she would be presented as Gabe's fiancée that afternoon, Sarah was still stunned.

The ring wasn't the old family jewel she had expected, borrowed for convenience. Made by a staggeringly exclusive jeweler, the oval-shaped sapphire rimmed with diamonds was modern and breathtakingly gorgeous.

Extracting the ring, Gabe picked up her left hand. "May I?"

Sarah blinked back ridiculously sentimental tears as he slipped the ring onto her third finger. It was a moment she had experienced twice before but which had never been more important or filled with emotion. "It's beautiful." And it fitted perfectly.

He opened the other flat velvet box, which contained equally gorgeous drop earrings and a pendant. "You'll need these, as well. After lunch, Faruq's arranged for one of the designer boutiques to outfit you for the press conference."

Still feeling a little misty, the businesslike necessity of the press conference grounded her. Sarah tucked the velvet boxes in her bag and minutes later they walked

out of the dim lower rooms and back into the airy lightness and clamor of the palace.

In the end, lunch with Gabe was canceled because
Faruq, a small quick man who looked more like an accountant than a marketing genius, insisted Sarah not only
needed an outfit, but that she must have her hair, nails
and makeup done. Hilary Kadir, who had joined them,
agreed to take Sarah to her stylist. Surrounded by palace staff, suddenly the responsibility Gabe carried hit
home. It explained his calm, measured manner, the lack
of outward emotion that sometimes felt like coldness.
She knew for a fact that he was neither cold nor emo-
tionless, but with cameras constantly pointed at him and
literally thousands of people dependent on him, he would
have learned early on to maintain that steely self-control.

Two hours of relentless pampering later, wearing a
slim-fitting royal blue jacket and skirt that deepened
the color of her eyes, her hair smoothed into a glossy,
thick swathe and tucked behind her ears to show off the
earrings, Sarah walked into the press conference with
Gabe. Already warned about the hot lights and the camera flashes, and prepped on what she should and should
not say, she did her best to keep her expression serene.

The questions came thick and fast, although Gabe
blocked most of them with a flat "No comment."

Thanks to the genius of Faruq, who had also briefed
the press beforehand and had plied them with champagne
and canapés, the sticky territory of their fling before
Gabe had gotten engaged to Nadia was barely touched
upon. Apparently, Nadia was now old news. The story
everyone wanted was the love affair between the sheikh

and the schoolteacher, a mismatch that carried echoes of Zahir's romantic past.

Annoyed by the idea that they were a mismatch, but bolstered by the positive atmosphere, Sarah allowed the beautiful ring to be photographed. When one of the journalists asked Gabe if he had finally gotten over Jasmine, and wanted to know what it felt like to be getting married again, Gabe pushed to his feet, pulling her with him. Thanking the press, his expression cold, he propelled her from the room.

A security guard fell into step behind them. When they reached Gabe's study, he took a call. His already grim expression turned icy. He glanced at Sarah, but seemed to barely see her. Curtly, he informed her that something urgent had come up then instructed the guard to see Sarah back to the cliff-top house.

As Sarah followed the guard out of the palace, the fact that Gabe had some emergency to cope with took second place to the question that was burned into her mind. The one that had abruptly ended the press conference and which she had hoped she had put behind her.

Was Gabe over Jasmine?

Fourteen

Sarah glanced in the rearview mirror as a sleek black sedan nosed out of the parking lot behind her. Feeling more and more upset as the minutes ticked by, Sarah pulled into the parking lot of the cliff house. She needed some air, without her guard, the six foot eight, Yusuf.

Changing into light jeans and a cotton camisole with a tight white cardigan buttoned over top, she checked to see where Yusuf had gone. When she heard his voice in the kitchen, she picked up her camera and bag and sneaked out a side door. When she reached the car, still in the clear, she turned the key in the ignition and pointed it down the drive. In her rearview mirror, she saw Yusuf race out onto the drive.

Adrenaline pumping, she turned onto the coast road. Her phone rang, but she didn't answer. Once she got to the bottom of the cliff, she would text the number he had given her before she had left the palace and let him know she would be an hour at most. A second turn and she was winding down the hill to the parking lot at the beach.

She drew a swift breath as Salamander Bay came into view, wild and beautiful and still almost devoid of habitation. As she brought the car to a halt in a parking lot occupied by half a dozen vehicles, she climbed from the car, feeling miserable, but consoled by the wildness of the spectacularly beautiful white sand beach with its high rock promontory that ran like a dark finger out to sea.

After texting Yusuf, she took a photo of the beach, which was occupied by sporadic bathers and the occasional bright umbrella. Turning, she took a shot of the rock promontory, which was brooding and spectacular, then she walked down onto the sand. She took a couple of snaps of the dark, brooding cliff face crowned by the fortress, which occupied the highest point in the bay, a square set against the onslaught of the wind with a sole crenellated tower.

Still feeling terminally unsettled because she was worried that Gabe was still in love with Jasmine, and that he wasn't willing to trust Sarah with that truth, she walked out along the rock promontory. The extra height gave her a better view of the beach and the place that was the wreck site of the *Salamander*. Sunlight glittering off polished metal caught her attention. A black sedan had just pulled into the parking lot.

She couldn't believe it when Graham emerged from the car and had the nerve to wave at her. She pretended not to see him and continued taking photos.

Irritated beyond belief that he seemed to find ways to insert himself into her life, she walked a little farther along the rocks. A wave, larger than any she'd yet seen, almost completely submerged the rocks ahead. Spray exploded, close enough to wet her. Suddenly aware of the danger and kicking herself for not being more careful, she tucked the camera in its the bag and started for shore.

Her stomach tightened as a flash of movement alerted her to the fact that someone was walking toward her. A curious sense of inevitability gripped her as she turned to see Gabe, still dressed in his formal suit. "Let me guess. Yusuf called you."

"You weren't supposed to leave the house without him." His gaze was trained steadily seaward. "Didn't you read the sign?"

"What sign?"

The sound of another large wave hitting rock spun her around, cold spray drenched her.

Gabe's arm snaked around her waist, steadying her. "The sign that said don't go out on the rocks." There was small, bleak silence. "This is where Jasmine died when her boat overturned."

The shock of his statement—of his finally mentioning Jasmine—was canceled out as the next wave flowed toward them, this one even larger. Fingers laced with hers, he pulled her onto a higher shelf of rock and back toward shore.

Breathless, Sarah worked to keep up with Gabe's smooth, gliding stride, glad that she was wearing sneakers and that she had kept up her walking during the pregnancy and was still reasonably fit. "I suppose people get swept off."

The wave broke sending more spray flying. The distraction took her attention from the uneven rock surface for a split second, making her wobble.

Gabe said something hard and sharp beneath his

breath as he reeled her in close again then swung her into his arms. "Not today."

Coiling her arms around his neck, she held on tight, worried that she had provided another painful reminder of Jasmine, but loving that Gabe had come to her rescue. Water dripped from his hair and clung to his lashes. His gaze rested on hers for a moment, the glint of masculine satisfaction sending a warm surge through her. She was soaked, they both were, but suddenly she didn't care. For a few moments they were alone, and like the hours they'd spent together last night, he was *hers*. "I'm sorry. I should have kept a better watch out. Graham arrived at the beach and I got a bit creeped out. I thought he would try and follow me."

Gabe's expression turned grim. "Don't worry about Southwell. Xavier has him under surveillance."

Resting her head in the curve of his neck and shoulder, she breathed in his warm scent. "I suppose that's how you found me? I ran into your secret service?"

She felt his smile rather than saw it. "What did you expect when you gave Yusuf the slip? Tell me, *kalila*, are you always this difficult?"

She was startled by his rueful expression, the softness of his gaze, as if he liked it that she was giving him such a hard time. "Only when I get engaged."

"And when you're pulling swords off displays, assaulting thugs with your umbrella and giving Tarik a hard time."

She blinked at the picture of herself. "Maybe I am difficult."

A curious expression crossed his face. "Don't change, I like it." Bending, he kissed her.

Her heart thumped at the kiss and the tone of his voice. "What does *kalila* mean?"

Stopping at the edge of the rock promontory where it flowed into the smooth, broad curve of the beach, he set her on her feet. "It's an endearment. On Zahir we use it much as you would honey or darling."

Feeling suddenly self-conscious, she smoothed wet straggling hair back from her cheeks. When his gaze flickered to her chest she glanced down and realized that her thin white cardigan and camisole were wet. Luckily, she had a bikini top beneath, so she could afford to ignore the wet T-shirt effect.

Gabe glanced along the cliff face. Graham was still there somewhere because his car was in the parking lot, although he was nowhere to be seen. At a guess he had disappeared into the warren of caves that riddled the rock.

When Gabe spoke his voice was terse. "I'm moving you into the palace tonight."

Gabe arranged for all of their belongings to be transferred to the palace.

Night was falling with a pretty sickle moon, the sky studded with brilliant stars as he drove into a cavernous garage beneath the palace.

He gave her a quick tour of the residential area, which used to be the old harem quarters and which had been remodeled into a series of family apartments. He pointed out where his parents stayed and two other empty apartments. "There are also a whole bunch of single and double rooms, but those are mostly empty unless family or guests come to stay."

He opened the door to their apartment and a warm

glow suffused her as she walked into the main sitting room, which was filled with comfortable leather couches and low coffee tables. A dining table was positioned in an alcove next to a gleaming kitchen. The dining table was set, candles lit, giving the room a welcoming elegance while the warm aromas of the meal that had been kept hot in silver chafing dishes drifted on the air.

Gabe gave her a quick tour. The next room, which Gabe indicated as they walked past, looked like a beautifully appointed guest room. That was followed by a large bathroom tiled in cream marble with a tub big enough to swim in.

She examined the large walk-in shower and the supply of fluffy white towels. "We'll have to block off the bathroom once the baby starts walking."

"Good point." He stared at the marble bath, which had steps that would be slippery when wet. "Even better, we'll get a house. This place is a death trap for kids."

The casual comment about getting a house made her heart glow with happiness. More and more they were starting to feel like a regular couple. She stepped inside what looked like the master bedroom, since it had its own bathroom and dressing room opening off it. This was confirmed by the masculine bedspread, the faint scent of Gabe's cologne and one of his shirts slung over the back of a chair.

Sarah checked out the dressing room, a faint tension she hadn't realized was there dissipating when she saw her suitcase. "I take it I'm staying in this room."

Gabe was leaning against the doorjamb watching her. "That's right, with me. Although, you can have the guest room if you want."

She strolled toward him and when he didn't move

aside she took another half step, which brought her up against him. She wound her fingers in the smooth silk of his tie. "I choose this room."

"I was hoping you were going to say that."

His phone hummed. Looking frustrated, he took the phone from his pocket, checked the screen and frowned. "I need to take this."

"No problem." While Gabe sat at a desk in a small study that opened off the lounge and took a series of calls, Sarah unpacked then had a quick shower to remove the salty residue from that afternoon. Toweling herself dry, she put on fresh underwear. Instead of dressing in the cotton shift she'd chosen, she decided to wear an exquisite rose-pink silk kaftan she had bought in the souk the morning Gabe had found her. The kaftan was gossamer fine and flowing but when belted with a silk sash became a gorgeous Eastern dress.

She combed out her hair and used the blow-dryer. When her hair was mostly dry and trailing down her back, she quickly applied a little eye makeup. Now that she finally knew how the makeup should look and what products to buy, she was determined not to go back to dashing on a bit of dark brown eyeliner and rose-pink lip gloss, both of which usually faded into invisibility within an hour.

Rummaging through her suitcase she found the pashmina that went with the outfit, an exquisitely fine woven cashmere stole in rich hues of purple and pink with splashes of deep red that added a sensual grace to the pretty kaftan. She examined the effect in the bathroom mirror. The outfit was more modest than the red dress she'd worn the night she'd met Gabe, there was only the barest hint of shadowy cleavage, yet somehow it was infinitely more feminine and mysterious.

With her hair dropping around her shoulders in a dark curtain, her eyes taking on a smoky, exotic slant courtesy of the eye shadow and mascara, she didn't look remotely like a sensible history teacher, neither did she feel like one anymore. The clothing seemed to underline the inner change that had taken place, almost without her being aware of it.

When she walked out into the lounge, Gabe was dishing up food. He must have had a shower in the other bathroom because his hair was damp and he'd changed into a pair of dark pants and a polo shirt. His gaze met hers as he set the plate he'd just filled on the table. Her pulse sped up at the intensity of his gaze as he took in the softly sensual outfit. "Are you hungry?"

"Starved."

They ate, although as delicious as the food was, Sarah could barely concentrate because she was so aware of Gabe.

When she was finished, he took her plate and set it in the sink in the kitchen, his expression taut. "Would you like dessert?"

She followed him and placed an empty salad bowl on the counter. "Not really."

"Me neither." With a grin, he picked her up and carried her through to the bedroom. "When you walked out of the bedroom like that, I didn't think I'd make it through dinner."

He set her on her feet. The Pashmina slid to the floor as she reached up to kiss him. One kiss followed another. She felt the silk sash loosen then slip off her shoulders and puddle at her feet. Two steps back and they were on the bed and somehow, this time, she was on top, her hair sliding silkily around them. Long drugging minutes later she was naked and so was Gabe.

Tension gripped her as she studied Gabe in the wash of light from the hall. For the first time, she was actually beginning to believe that he could be hers.

Cupping his face, she looked directly into his eyes. "I love you." The words were bald and declarative, leaving her nowhere to hide.

Instead of the words she wanted in return, she felt his instant tension and knew she shouldn't have made the declaration, shouldn't have pushed him. Even if he had mentioned Jasmine today, it was still too soon. A split second later, he kissed her and, determined not to fret, she relaxed into the kiss and let the warmth and heat of lovemaking encompass them both.

A phone call in the early hours brought Sarah out of a deep, dreamless sleep. Rolling over in bed, she slipped an arm around Gabe's taut waist as he lay, propped on one elbow, speaking in rapid Zahiri. When he hung up, the gray light of dawn illuminated the grim expression on his face. "That was Xavier. They've been keeping Southwell under surveillance. Apparently, he's found the lost dowry, which was sealed in a side cave in Salamander Bay. That's what he was doing there today, re-packing the caskets and getting ready to transport them to the loading docks at the port where he has an export container waiting." Expression taut, Gabe set the phone down. "Damn Southwell and the dowry. Why did he have to find it *now*?"

Climbing out of bed, Gabe dressed and was gone within minutes.

Unable to go back to sleep, Sarah belted on the beautiful silk kaftan, freshened up in the bathroom then walked through to the sitting room. Gabe's words kept echoing through her mind.

Damn Southwell and the dowry. Why did he have to find it now?

As if Gabe had wished the dowry had been found some other time. Probably months ago, a year ago, so he would never have given way to the pressure of an arranged marriage in the first place. Because if that hadn't happened, he would never have spent a dangerous night of passion with her that had resulted in a pregnancy, and what could only be termed a marriage of convenience.

Dragging fingers through her tangled hair, she paced through the huge apartment, strolling through moonlit rooms only to find herself in Gabe's study, the one room she hadn't seen on their tour. Curious, she flicked on a light and strolled to tall French doors and looked out onto a beautiful patio. When she turned, she noted a rich leather photograph album on top of a polished mahogany desk.

Knowing that she shouldn't, she flipped the album open. The first section had Gabe and Jasmine's engagement photos. Lavish wedding shots followed and the final section was filled with romantic honeymoon photos. Feeling a little sick, because Jasmine looked glowingly happy in every photo, her arms either draped around Gabe's neck or his waist, as if she couldn't bear not to touch him.

She closed the album with a snap. As she did so, she noticed a folder beside it, carrying her name.

Feeling like an automaton, she picked up the file and opened it. Fifteen minutes later, feeling sick, she set the file back in its place. She had known that Gabe had had her investigated, but this file was a detailed *surveillance* record that Gabe had ordered after their first night together. He had expressly stated that he wanted her watched in case she was pregnant.

Seeing the truth about how Gabe had viewed her, in stark contrast to his romantic, loving relationship with Jasmine, was hard to take. It *hurt*.

She guessed that, given he was a sheikh's son and the future ruler of Zahir, she could understand his approach. But that didn't change the fact that she had given up everything for Gabe, including her heart, and he had given up very little for her. He still hadn't shared even the bare facts about his marriage.

Feeling numb, she replaced the file. As understanding as she had tried to be, she wasn't stupid, she had limits, and her limits had just been breached.

She had taken a risk in loving Gabe, moving in with him and agreeing to marriage. She knew he'd been hurt in the past, but even so she had believed there was a possibility that he would come to love her someday.

But she couldn't stomach marriage on such compromised terms, with someone who had seen her as predatory. It underlined the fact that if she hadn't gotten pregnant and forced his hand, she would never have seen Gabe again.

Face burning at the humiliation of seeing the basis of their relationship laid bare, of having her life sifted through, *by the man she loved*, she left the study and found her way back to the bedroom. Their bedroom, but not any longer.

Lamplight pooled like liquid gold, casting a soft glow on the beautiful plastered walls and delicate frescoes.

Chest tight, she opened a set of doors and stepped onto the balcony, staring out over the moonlit city to the sea. It was all unspeakably beautiful and she loved it, but she was going to have to leave.

She finally understood why Gabe had agreed to a marriage of convenience to Nadia and why he'd never confided in her about his past with Jasmine. It was because he didn't want the one thing she craved: intimacy.

The moment was defining. She had said she would marry Gabe, but how could she when his heart wasn't in it? When his heart might *never* be in it?

She knew what it felt like to be second best, to be passed over. It hadn't been a good feeling, but she had gotten over it. She didn't think she could get over Gabe, but neither would she be second best for him.

She had always thought she was lacking in passion, but when Gabe had entered her life she had discovered that she was passionate and volatile. She wanted a real love with Gabe with a fierceness that shimmered and burned and made her want to cry.

Knowing now that she would never have his love, she had to act. When she had the baby Gabe would love their daughter and want to be a father to her, but that was a scenario with a modern solution. He might not like the idea, but the only sensible thing to do was to share custody.

Working quickly, she retrieved her bags from the closet. She didn't know how much time she had before Gabe returned, so she simply stuffed clothing into them. She found her engagement ring, which she'd left on the bedside table, and replaced it in its velvet case. She put the case along with the second case containing the pendant and earrings on the dressing table. On impulse, she walked through to Gabe's study, found the photo album and the surveillance report and placed them beside the jewelry boxes.

She checked her watch. An hour had flown by. She needed to leave before she weakened and changed her mind.

Gabe would hate it that she'd walked out on him. He was an alpha male. But the very strengths that made him such a good leader were the qualities that would push them apart in the end. He would continue to sacrifice his free choice, and perhaps his happiness, and she couldn't bear that.

Walking through to the bathroom, she splashed cold water on her face. Feeling chilled despite the balmy warmth, she used her cell to call a local taxi firm and arranged to meet the cab in the residential street that backed onto the palace grounds.

Fumbling slightly in her haste, she changed into cotton jeans and a sweater and pulled on sneakers. She found a scarf and on impulse used it to cover her hair, tying it under her chin. After all the media coverage she was now recognizable on Zahir. It wasn't much of a disguise, but it would have to do.

She carried the luggage downstairs and outside to the street, leaving it in the shadow of a huge flowering rhododendron. Walking back to the apartment, she did a last check of the rooms, picked up her handbag, hooked the strap over her shoulder and walked out onto the landing. Headlights beamed up the driveway. Heart in her mouth, feeling sick to her stomach at what she was doing, Sarah walked quickly down the stairs.

Fifteen

Gabe locked the car and headed for the stairs. Now that the situation with Southwell and the dowry was resolved, with Southwell in custody and the dowry in safekeeping, all Gabe wanted was to go back to bed with Sarah and preserve what time they had before the major news companies picked up on the story and all hell broke loose.

Faruq was coordinating the press releases. With any luck, he would finesse the timing of the discovery of the ancient treasure as a "sign" that the marriage to Sarah was propitious for Zahir. The romantic tale of his ancestor's love affair with Camille de Vallois would do the rest.

As Gabe stepped inside the apartment, the curious quality of the silence made him frown. Somewhere outside he heard a car door close, the sound of an engine. On edge he walked into the bedroom. Moonlight slanted over the rumpled bed, which was empty. Stomach tight, he checked the bathroom, which was also empty.

Out of the corner of his eye he saw the two velvet cases on the dresser and the photograph album and surveillance report he had left on his desk with the intention of destroying them that morning.

He went cold inside. For the album and the file to be where they were, Sarah had clearly found and perused them. A quick glance in the spare room confirmed that Sarah hadn't just moved out of his bedroom. She had left him.

For long moments he couldn't think. Then he remembered the slamming of the car door out in the street. Sarah must have called a taxi.

Heart slamming against the wall of his chest, he picked up the phone, called Xavier and arranged to detain her at the airport.

With distaste, he forced himself to look at one of Jasmine's last gifts to him, an album filled with photos that portrayed a love story that had grown to be cloying and unhealthy.

Jaw taut, he opened the surveillance file and skimmed the damning evidence of his letter requesting a watch on Sarah in case she was pregnant. The report included an extensive back history on Sarah's life because for some reason Tarik had gotten a little overzealous and had requested the private investigator dig back several years.

Reading through the bare facts, Sarah had looked like a woman who had amassed a certain experience with men, but Gabe knew the truth. The reason none of the relationships had stuck was because she had refused to sleep with them. But she had slept with him, after little more than a few hours.

Because she had fallen in love with him.

Grimly, he remembered her saying the words to him tonight, his complete lack of response because, even then, in a sheer knee-jerk reaction he had automatically closed himself off.

She loved him.

He felt like he'd been kicked in the chest. Sarah wasn't like Jasmine, wavering with every breeze, clinging and resenting at the same time and wanting to be spoiled and cosseted. She was independent and fierce. Used to making her own way through life, for years she had refused to give in to relationship pressure and have sex. She had waited and chosen, and she had chosen him.

Once she had found she was pregnant, she hadn't panicked. She had gone in search of him, not to coerce him into a relationship, but to ascertain whether she should include him in her life. Those were the actions of a rational, independent woman who had fallen in love.

Tossing the report down on the desk, he found his keys and headed for his car. He felt electrified, every nerve ending in his body on fire. Sarah had told him, but now he knew in his gut—and his heart—exactly why she had agreed to marry him, and why she had left. She loved him but she had given up on the hope that he could love her back.

And suddenly he realized what he had done to himself, and to Sarah. After Jasmine had died he had spent years consumed by guilt, not because he had failed to save her life, but because he had never been able to *love her*.

He and Jasmine had been wrong together and that tension had reverberated through their marriage, ending in a tragedy that he had allowed to color the rest of his life.

Panic gripped him. He felt as if the scales had just been ripped from his eyes. Too late, he now realized that he did love Sarah. And now he had lost her.

He was partway to the airport when he knew it was the wrong destination. Sarah was smart. She would have known how easy it would be for him to stop her flying.

Turning the car around, he headed for the ferry terminal, the only other way off Zahir other than chartering a yacht or boarding a cruise ship. There were no cruise ships leaving today, and chartering a yacht was a lengthy process because it involved customs declarations. Boarding a ferry to the neighboring island of Al Jahir was a much simpler option.

His stomach churned at the thought that she had chosen the sea as a way to escape him. *Jasmine's choice.*

As he drove he went through every nuance of their last conversation, which had been about the dowry. He knew that, like him, Sarah placed no stock in money or possessions. Southwell had chased the treasure for its own sake, but Sarah, who should have been more interested in it than most with her family background, had barely shown a flicker of interest.

From memory the only thing about the past that had interested her had been whether or not his ancestor had loved hers.

His fingers tightened on the wheel as he turned down the street that led to the docks. Jaw tight, he found a space and slammed out of the car. Sarah was simple and declarative. She had told him she loved him, but he had failed to reciprocate. He had taken the easy way out, *the cowardly way out*, because then he didn't have to expose his own emotions. He didn't have to take any risks.

That would have to change; he couldn't lose her.

Gabe faced the raw depth of emotions that in the past had caused him more pain than happiness.

He wouldn't let Sarah go without a fight.

Sarah boarded the early-morning ferry to Al Jahir.

Stepping inside the lower deck cabin, which was already half-filled with passengers drinking coffee and watching TV, Sarah made a beeline for a seat near a window. She stopped when she noticed a large TV was on and that the coverage riveting most of the passengers was a news story on the crates of gold and jewels that Graham had tried to steal.

In no mood to listen to the story she was on the point of walking out onto the ferry deck when Gabe's deep voice kept her riveted to the screen. She recognized footage of an earlier interview that had been linked with the segment about the dowry, but even so, when Gabe was asked about his impending marriage his curt "no comment" stung.

The reporter smoothed over the awkwardness of the moment by stating that in Zahir any marriage by the ruling family was necessarily an affair of state.

Shivering slightly and hugging her cotton jersey closer against her skin, she walked to the upper deck and ducked inside out of the brisk wind. She stared through one of the large windows at the palace, which gleamed in the first golden touches of morning light, and the terraced jumble of streets and villas that gave Zahir such charm. Feeling miserable, she forced herself to look in the direction of Al Jahir, a misty lump on the horizon. She had made the right decision, even if it made her feel ill.

She was tired, so she bought a cup of tea from the

small cafeteria. She guessed she should eat something, but her stomach was still churning and unsettled, and the faint wallow of the sea swell wasn't helping.

She chose a seat that overlooked the docks, just in case Gabe arrived before the ferry left. She hoped he wouldn't come after her because if he did she didn't know if she'd have the strength to resist him.

Gabe walked inside the ferry building. He had missed the sailing by about twenty minutes. He could still see the ferry in the distance. He asked to see the manifest. His jaw tightened when he spotted Sarah's name.

Thanking the clerk, he left the building and made a call. Al Jahir was ruled by his cousin several times removed, Kalil. The relationship was distant, but that didn't matter. They were family. A second call and he had arranged a helicopter.

Half an hour later he landed on the docks of Al Jahir. When the ferry anchored just offshore, embargoed from landing until he had retrieved Sarah, Gabe took the launch Kalil had provided and climbed on board.

When Sarah saw him, her stricken expression gave him a small measure of hope. Although, he had mishandled their relationship so badly he had to wonder if he had finally destroyed her love.

Ignoring the disgruntled crowd of ferry passengers, he concentrated on Sarah. "Will you come with me?"

She shot to her feet, clutching her handbag. "Why?"

"Because you belong on Zahir, with me."

The sleepy-eyed tourist next to her muttered, "Last I heard slavery went out of fashion a few years back."

Someone else grunted agreement and added, "*And* piracy. Honey, if you need backup just say the word."

Jaw locked, Gabe kept his focus on Sarah. "You're free to leave anytime. But I need you to hear me out, in private."

Minutes later, caught halfway between misery and delight that Gabe had come after her, Sarah allowed Gabe to hand her down into the launch.

A short helicopter ride and they landed on the roof of the palace, which had a helipad.

As Sarah walked back into the familiarity of Gabe's apartment, her stomach tightened. "I left because I didn't want you to feel you had to marry me just to have access to the baby." She lifted her chin. "You're her father, so it's only right that you should have a part in her upbringing. We just need to reach agreement on how that will work."

Gabe shrugged out of his jacket and tossed it over the back of a chair. He ran lean fingers through his hair, looking suddenly unutterably weary. "Zahir is an old-fashioned country. The only agreement that will work here is marriage, and that's what I want."

She blinked at the intensity of his gaze. "I found the surveillance report."

His expression turned raw. "It was something I had to do, because I knew I couldn't afford to contact you again unless there was a child. If I hadn't instigated the report, Xavier would have. At least that way I could make sure the information came only to me and ensure your privacy."

The tension when she had discovered the report relaxed a little. She still hated that she'd been spied upon, but viewed that way, Gabe's actions had a protective element. "I thought you hated it that you were being forced to marry at all. If the dowry had been found months ago—"

"I would never have gotten engaged to Nadia. And since I was always going to New Zealand for the promotional tour our relationship would probably have followed a more normal path."

She stared at a pulse jumping along the side of his jaw. "But, when Graham found the dowry—"

"I was annoyed because I'd finally gotten you to myself, and then Southwell put himself in the frame again." He grimaced. "In case you hadn't noticed the dowry is a media circus. I knew I'd be out for hours."

Sarah took a deep breath. She was starting to feel happy, but she couldn't allow herself to relax just yet. "What about Jasmine?"

"I married Jasmine because I thought I loved her, but that was years ago."

The words *thought I loved her* seemed to reverberate. Her throat closed up so that when she spoke the words came out in a husky croak. "Do you still love her?"

Something cleared in his expression. "She was a childhood sweetheart. The media blew it up into a big love affair, but the marriage was a mistake. Jasmine was stuck on Zahir while I traveled. She hated it."

In terse, halting words he supplied a brief outline of the day Jasmine had drowned. He'd been spending more and more time away on business, tired of the fights and Jasmine's unhappiness. When Jasmine had insisted on accompanying him on a diving trip he had let her and when another fiery argument had ensued, he had suggested they end the marriage. Jasmine had lost her temper and in desperation had clung to him. Tired of her manipulative tactics and the clinging, he had gone below to study the navigation maps. When he had come back on deck, Jasmine, who had never handled a boat in her life, had taken the small dinghy, determined to row to shore. The dinghy had been swept onto a rock shelf and the boat had capsized on top of her. Gabe had dove down to search for her.

Sarah touched his cheek. "And that's how you got this."

His hand covered hers, holding it against the scar. "I had to get her off the rocks."

And the scar had become a permanent reminder that he hadn't been able to save his wife—more, that he had no longer loved her. It was no wonder he hadn't wanted anything to do with love again. "You can't believe it was your fault."

"I shouldn't have argued with her on the boat."

"And she shouldn't have taken the dinghy." Sarah unlocked her jaw. "I'm sorry she died, but it's a fact that she endangered your life as well as her own."

By the startled acknowledgment in his eyes she knew he hadn't considered that angle, preferring to take all the blame on his own shoulders. The only problem was that the guilt had morphed into an aversion toward emotional commitment that had almost destroyed their chance at love.

He threaded his fingers through hers, pulling her closer. "When it came to you, I knew I was in trouble, but I tried to channel the emotion into a purely sexual connection. It didn't work."

"Then I got pregnant." And he had attempted to transfer the "safe" relationship model he had settled on to her, and that hadn't worked either.

She cupped his jaw, suddenly seeing him, his tenderness and depth. "Even though I was a lot of trouble, you didn't let me go." She tried to breathe deeply, but her chest felt banded and tight. "Why?"

His hands closed around her arms, his palms warm through the cotton pullover. "That would be because I'm in love with you."

Happiness flared deep inside. Not just love, but *in love*. "Since when?"

"Since the moment I saw you completely ignore the don't-touch sign and knock my ancestor's sword to the floor." He pulled her snug against him. "I suppose you think because I'm a guy I'm incapable of that kind of depth."

She spread her palms over the warm solidity of his chest, loving the steady beat of his heart, the heat and strength of him. "It was a fact that I was a last fling before you got engaged." Flickers of the old hurt came back to haunt her at the words.

"I was on the point of getting engaged. It was an arrangement that had taken months to negotiate then I blew it by sleeping with you. That should tell you something."

She went still inside. Somewhere in all of this she realized she had lost the ability to stand back and look at the big picture, or to read between the lines. The one thing she had learned about Gabe was that for most of his adult life he had put Zahir ahead of his own wants and desires. The only times he had departed from that pattern were when he had married Jasmine, then again when he had slept with Sarah.

She stared at the clean, strong planes and angles of his face, the steadiness of his gaze. "You really did fall for me."

He cupped her face, his thumbs drifting over her

cheekbones, giving her goose bumps. "Like a ton of bricks."

"The way I fell for you."

His gaze connected with hers in a poignant moment of recognition.

She coiled her arms around his neck, holding him tight, loving the rock-solid quality that had frustrated her so often but which carried its own assurance. She knew without doubt that she and their daughter could trust Gabe with their hearts.

They had finally come home.

Sixteen

They didn't delay the wedding, even though Gabe was happy to do so. Sarah, now secure in his love, decided she had to do her bit for Zahir, and upsetting the travel plans of hundreds of people wasn't a good way to start.

The next day Gabe ushered Sarah into his study, where Faruq was impatiently waiting to find out just how the new wedding would affect his promotional efforts.

He was visibly relieved when Sarah informed him she was prepared to accept the current wedding date. She fixed him with the calm, level look she used in the classroom. "But I'm not getting married in the dead of night, like it's some kind of secret—"

"It's hardly a secret with four hundred guests."

Sarah frowned at the interruption. "—since it's my wedding." She softened the statement with a blinding smile that, to Gabe's mind, seemed to light up the room.

"Also," she continued, "I want my cousin Laine's son to be a page and her three daughters to be flower girls. Since they're family, and on the next island, that should happen."

Sarah kept her attention on Faruq as he took notes. "I'm thinking one o'clock is a good time for the ceremony. Midnight might have suited Nadia, but it doesn't suit me or my nephew or nieces. Laine's youngest has only just started to sleep through the night. You can't expect us to upset that pattern when it's taken so long to put in place."

Faruq looked suitably chastened. "Uh—of course not—"

"Good." She sent him an affirming smile. "It's also crucially important that people should understand that Gabe is not being *forced* to marry me."

Gabe hid a grin.

"Um—I don't think Sheikh Kadin was being forced as such, it was more of a service to the country."

"With a financial benefit." Sarah favored Faruq with another brilliant smile. "My point exactly. Gabe is not marrying me for money. He's marrying me because—"

"You're irresistible to him." Gabe thought he would just toss that one in.

Sarah's gaze locked with his. "Irresistible?"

Gabe pulled her into his arms. "Absolutely."

When she went up on her toes and rewarded him with a kiss, he heard the door close softly as Faruq let himself out. The meeting had ended a little precipitately, but it didn't matter. Faruq was a creative genius and he was already excited about the promotional potential in Gabe's marriage to a descendant of Camille, especially when combined with the recovery of the ancient dowry.

According to Faruq those two aspects could only enhance Zahir's new image as a destination for romantic getaways, and would make it relatively easy to gloss over the small detail that Gabe and Sarah had already made a start on a family. For Zahir the formula was win-win, but for Gabe those two elements held little importance to him when he finally had what he wanted—the gorgeous, fascinating love of his life and their first child together.

The day of the wedding dawned fine and clear. The ceremony was held in the ancient stone church next door to the palace. Golden sunlight poured through the rose window at the western end. Jewel-bright colors illuminated thick flagstones and the gleam of dark oak pews. The church overflowed with guests, so seats had been placed outside along with two very modern screens with speakers.

A restive murmur ran through the guests as Gabe's parents arrived and took their places. His father looked tanned and relaxed after a recent holiday and was no longer walking with the aid of a cane. His mother looked elegant and happier than he had seen her for years. She sent Gabe a beaming smile and a small thumbs-up.

Although Gabe couldn't quite relax until Sarah arrived. It was an insecurity that shouldn't have existed after the days and nights they'd spent together, but he couldn't quite forget the stark moment when he'd found out she'd left him just weeks ago.

Xavier checked his watch and frowned. "She's late."

"Tradition." Gabe's gaze was drawn to the priest, robed in white, as he also checked his watch. "Probably caught up in traffic."

The noise level outside increased. An usher at the front doors gave Gabe a nod. He let out a breath and relaxed. She was here.

Sarah stepped into the church, a little frazzled after the frustration of sitting in the back of a limousine that seemed to spend large amounts of time stuck in heavy traffic or at a standstill because of the crush of pedestrians. All wanting to get to *her* wedding.

A liltingly beautiful wedding march started, and the hum of conversation died. Gabe turned, looking tall and handsome in a gray morning suit and wearing the traditional *kaffiyeh* and *agal*. His gaze connected with hers through the drift of her veil. The quiet joy that he was hers seemed to swell inside her, forming an ache at the back of her throat.

Gripping the elegant bouquet that matched the simple lines of her designer gown, she began the slow, measured walk toward her husband-to-be.

With every step memories flickered. Gabe straightening with the sword in his hand at the reception in Wellington, the rescue in the parking lot, their first kiss, the first night they had spent together.

Blinking back tears, she halted at the ancient altar, which had seen the flow of centuries, bowed her head, made the sign of the cross and turned to her husband-to-be.

Sheikh Kadin Gabriel ben Kadir, heir to the Sheikhdom of Zahir.

For a moment, her composure wobbled, but when he lifted the veil from her face and took her hands in his, the warmth of his gaze held her steady.

The hush of the church, the beauty of the words of the

ceremony, filled her with an emotion that was piercing. When Gabe slipped the simple gold band on her finger, tears finally spilled.

His mouth brushed hers; his hands at her waist burned through the silk of her gown. Beeswax candles guttered in the faint breeze that blew through windows and suddenly the air was filled with the wild sweet scents of honey and thyme.

Sarah's head spun dizzily as she went up on her toes to kiss him back.

She finally had it all, more than she had ever dreamed— the father of her child and the love she had waited for, the husband of her heart.

* * * * *

If you loved this book from
Fiona Brand,
pick up the novels in her PEARL HOUSE *series*

A BREATHLESS BRIDE
A TANGLED AFFAIR
A PERFECT HUSBAND
THE FIANCÉE CHARADE
JUST ONE MORE NIGHT

Available now from Harlequin Desire!

If you're on Twitter, tell us what you think of
Harlequin Desire! #harlequindesire

COMING NEXT MONTH FROM

HARLEQUIN® *Desire*

Available June 2, 2015

#2377 WHAT THE PRINCE WANTS
Billionaires and Babies • by Jules Bennett
Needing time to heal, a widowed prince goes incognito. He hires a live-in nanny for his infant daughter but soon finds he wants the woman for *himself*. Is he willing to cross the line from professional to personal?

#2378 CARRYING A KING'S CHILD
Dynasties: The Montoros • by Katherine Garbera
Torn between running his family's billion-dollar shipping business and assuming his ancestral throne, Rafe Montoro needs to let off some steam. But his night with a bartending beauty could change everything—because now there's a baby on the way...

#2379 PURSUED BY THE RICH RANCHER
Diamonds in the Rough • by Catherine Mann
Driven by his grandmother's dying wish, a Texas rancher must choose between his legacy and the sexy single mother who unknowingly holds the fate of his heart—and his inheritance—in her hands.

#2380 THE SHEIKH'S SECRET HEIR
by Kristi Gold
Billionaire Tarek Azzmar knows a secret that will destroy the royal family who shunned him. But the tables turn when he learns his lover is near and dear to the royal family *and* she's pregnant with his child.

#2381 THE WIFE HE COULDN'T FORGET
by Yvonne Lindsay
Olivia Jackson steals a second chance with her estranged husband when he loses his memories of the past two years. But when he finally remembers *everything*, will their reconciliation stand the ultimate test?

#2382 SEDUCED BY THE CEO
Chicago Sons • by Barbara Dunlop
When businessman Riley Ellis learns that his rival's wife has a secret twin sister, he seduces the beauty as leverage and then hires her to keep her close. But now he's trapped by his own lies...and his desires...

REQUEST YOUR FREE BOOKS!
2 FREE NOVELS PLUS 2 FREE GIFTS!

HARLEQUIN®

Desire

ALWAYS POWERFUL, PASSIONATE AND PROVOCATIVE

YES! Please send me 2 FREE Harlequin® Desire novels and my 2 FREE gifts (gifts are worth about $10). After receiving them, if I don't wish to receive any more books, I can return the shipping statement marked "cancel." If I don't cancel, I will receive 6 brand-new novels every month and be billed just $4.55 per book in the U.S. or $5.24 per book in Canada. That's a savings of at least 13% off the cover price! It's quite a bargain! Shipping and handling is just 50¢ per book in the U.S. and 75¢ per book in Canada.* I understand that accepting the 2 free books and gifts places me under no obligation to buy anything. I can always return a shipment and cancel at any time. Even if I never buy another book, the two free books and gifts are mine to keep forever.

225/326 HDN GH2P

Name _____ (PLEASE PRINT) _____

Address _____ Apt. # _____

City _____ State/Prov. _____ Zip/Postal Code _____

Signature (if under 18, a parent or guardian must sign)

Mail to the **Reader Service**:
IN U.S.A.: P.O. Box 1867, Buffalo, NY 14240-1867
IN CANADA: P.O. Box 609, Fort Erie, Ontario L2A 5X3

Want to try two free books from another line?
Call 1-800-873-8635 or visit www.ReaderService.com.

* Terms and prices subject to change without notice. Prices do not include applicable taxes. Sales tax applicable in N.Y. Canadian residents will be charged applicable taxes. Offer not valid in Quebec. This offer is limited to one order per household. Not valid for current subscribers to Harlequin Desire books. All orders subject to credit approval. Credit or debit balances in a customer's account(s) may be offset by any other outstanding balance owed by or to the customer. Please allow 4 to 6 weeks for delivery. Offer available while quantities last.

Your Privacy—The Reader Service is committed to protecting your privacy. Our Privacy Policy is available online at www.ReaderService.com or upon request from the Reader Service.

We make a portion of our mailing list available to reputable third parties that offer products we believe may interest you. If you prefer that we not exchange your name with third parties, or if you wish to clarify or modify your communication preferences, please visit us at www.ReaderService.com/consumerchoice or write to us at Reader Service Preference Service, P.O. Box 9062, Buffalo, NY 14240-9062. Include your complete name and address.

HD15

Pregnant!

He knew Emily wouldn't be standing in his penthouse apartment telling him this if he wasn't the father. His first reaction was joy.

A child.

It wasn't something he'd ever thought he wanted, but the idea that Emily was carrying his baby seemed right to him.

Maybe that was just because it gave him something other than his royal duties to think about. He'd been dreading his trip to Alma. He was flattered that the country that had once driven his family out had come back to them, asked them—him, as it turned out—to be the next king. But he had grown up here in Miami. He didn't want to be a stuffy royal.

He didn't want European paparazzi following him around and trying to catch him doing anything that would bring shame to his family. Including having a child out of wedlock.

"Yeah, I did. Are you sure?" he asked at last.

She gave him a fiery look from those aqua-blue eyes of hers. He'd seen the passionate side of her nature, and he guessed he was about to witness her temper. Hurricane Em was about to unleash all of her fury on him, and he didn't blame her one bit.

He held his hand up. "Slow down, Red. I didn't mean are you sure it's mine. I meant...are you sure you're pregnant?"

"Damned straight. And I wouldn't be here if I wasn't sure it was yours. Listen, I don't want anything from you. I know you can't turn your back on your family and marry me, and frankly, we only had one weekend together, so I'd have to say no to a proposal anyway. But...I don't want this kid to grow up without knowing you."

"Me neither."

She glanced up, surprised.

He'd sort of surprised himself. But it didn't seem right for a kid of his to grow up without him. He wanted that. He wanted a chance to impart the Montoro legacy...not the one newly sprung on him involving a throne, but the one he'd carved for himself in business. "Don't look shocked."

"You've kind of got a lot going on right now. And having a kid with me isn't going to go over well."

"Tough," he said. "I still make my own decisions."

Available June 2015 wherever
Harlequin® Desire books and ebooks are sold.

www.Harlequin.com

THE WORLD IS BETTER WITH

Romance

Harlequin has everything from contemporary, passionate and heartwarming to suspenseful and inspirational stories.

Whatever your mood, we have a romance just for you!

Connect with us to find your next great read, special offers and more.

f /HarlequinBooks

🐦 @HarlequinBooks

www.HarlequinBlog.com

www.Harlequin.com/Newsletters

◆H HARLEQUIN®

A *Romance* FOR EVERY MOOD™